is this real?

real? a

. YES

DEAD INSIDE
DO NOT ENTER

NOTES FROM THE ZOMBIE APOCALYPSE

A Lost Zombies Book

CHRONICLE BOOKS

SAN FRANCISCO

This book is dedicated to the members of lostzombies.com. Without you, none of this would be possible.

Contributors:

The Lost Zombies Community	Greg "Laz" Lazenby	Pam Cornacchione
Adrian Chappell	Hailey Leach	Poe
Alexandra Fregoso	James Martinez	Rob Reault
April Whitney	Jason Lind	Sarah Mankowski
Becca Cohen	Jillian Naylor	Scot Lundy
Beth Maloney	Joseph Montes	Stephen "Stevi" Moore
Dylan Worthey	Kemarie Kurtz	Stephen "Majhi" Rhinehart
Eliza	Kim Romero	Steve Mockus
Emilie Sandoz	Lauren Lind	T.H. Theimer Jr.
Envidium	Levi Walton	Victoria Thomas
Erin Willis	Mary Lee Evelyn Keeney	William Bruin
Gary "G" Hardwick	Monkey Butt Films	ZombieJack

Library of Congress Cataloging-in-Publication Data

Dead inside : do not enter : notes from the zombie apocalypse
p. cm.

ISBN 978-1-4521-0108-8 (pbk.)

1. Zombies—Fiction. 2. Epidemics—Fiction. 3. Horror tales, American.

PS648.Z64D43 2011
813'.0873808—dc23

2011016488

Manufactured in China

Typesetting by Suzanne LaGasa

10 9 8 7 6 5 4 3 2 1

Chronicle Books LLC
680 Second Street
San Francisco, CA 94107
www.chroniclebooks.com

Editor's Note

The contents presented in this book were originally discovered in a backpack in the town of Colfax, located in Northern California. It is presumed that the last owner of the backpack is the author of the notes on pages 8 through 10. He or she seems to have acquired the notes, letters, and photographs having already been previously collected and may or may not have added further to the collection. It's also unclear how many people may have carried the backpack and added to the collection before it reached the author of these most recent notes. It is clear that those who kept the collection considered it an important enough record to carry, even while other survival factors would have weighed against doing so.

The material is presented here unaltered and as it was removed from the backpack.

Timeline

February—The Super Flu

The so-called super flu pandemic begins in February as a common, seasonal influenza. By March, the number of cases reported has quadrupled, and the flu strain is first dubbed "the super flu" by the media. The super flu proves resistant to influenza vaccines. On April 1st, the World Health Organization announces that the super flu meets the three criteria of a pandemic. In the streets, people begin wearing dust and surgical masks. As May approaches, there is still no vaccine for the flu strain. The public directs blame at the U.S. government, and there are protests in cities across the United States. In San Francisco, a man robs a bank with a squirt bottle full of what he claims is super flu–infected blood.

January   February   March   April   May   June

May—Camp St. Teresa

On May 1st, the U.S. government, working through FEMA and the CDC, sets up a camp in the Nevada desert with the announced purpose of treating the uninsured sick. The government issues St. Teresa "passports" to hospitals across the country. Hospital staffs are instructed to give the passports, which grant access to Camp St. Teresa, to uninsured patients in need. People all over the country rush to their local hospitals seeking passports. By June 1st, all the passports have been issued, and a black market for real and counterfeit passports flourishes. By mid June, additional camps are set up in every state across the country. Each of those is full by the end of June.

July—The Campion Virus

Thirty-five-year-old Russell Campion is discovered to have a mutated strain of the virus. The mutated flu spreads, and the total death toll doubles in just a few weeks, from 50,000 to over 100,000. The CDC dubs the mutated super flu "the Campion virus." Cases of the mutation are documented around the world. The United Nations declares a global state of emergency. Accounts surface from Camp St. Teresa that describe dire living conditions, as well as reports that the facility is in fact a "death camp," where the infected are sent to die. The government characterizes the purpose of St. Teresa and other camps as "quarantine." Widespread rioting occurs. On July 14th, protesters set fire to the U.S. capitol building and martial law is enacted.

September—Dead and Attacking

On September 8th, an emergency call is placed from a mobile phone somewhere near the city of Davis in Northern California. The person making the call claims that he is at a pharmaceutical testing facility where they are testing Campion virus treatments. The caller claims that some of the patients have died and are attacking people. The emergency services operator asks if the patients are dead or are attacking, to which the caller responds, "Both." This is the first recorded case of zombie behavior resulting from the Campion virus.

November—"We Lost Some Zombies"

On November 1st, the headline on New York's leading newspaper reads "We Lost Some Zombies." The quote is from a uniformed guard stationed at Camp St. Teresa, excerpted from a frantic radio transmission made by the guard before he and other soldiers flee the facility in Humvees. By November 2nd, the infected reach Las Vegas. Despite a significant army presence and efforts to quarantine the city, it falls within days, and the infection spreads across the entire continent by November 7th. There is no way to know for certain, but it is estimated that 75 percent of the population is dead or undead by November 19th. Governments collapse. Cities have largely gone dark, outside of the power from isolated civic and private generators. Survivors around the world are left largely on their own.

July	August	September	October	November	December

August—A New Industry

By August, pharmaceutical companies claiming to have a cure for the Campion virus begin selling their products directly to consumers and drug stores, circumventing any regulatory or approval process. The benefits of the drugs are unproven, and in light of events to come, functionally nonexistent.

Present Day

The only way to contract the virus is by bite. Infection results in zombification in all cases but does not always result in death. A still-living person infected with the Campion virus may turn into a zombie without dying; these infected do not retain the cognitive abilities held in life but do keep a greater measure of their physical abilities and strength than those who turn after death. They are called "runners."

Jacob, I know you'll find this.
You'll want to know what happened.
Well I can tell you that it's not
worth knowing. And if you think
I'm hiding something from you
you're right. Don't get sensitive
about it. I can picture you, shaking
your goddamn fist, asking what
the fuck is wrong with me. there's
a lot wrong. Very, very, wrong.
I've done some bad things. Stuff
I don't want to remember.

How I found these things. I shot a kid.
She was maybe 10. The things, I don't
know if this was good or bad. She was bit.
Not one of them yet, but bit all the same. She
was scared. Not because it hurt. She was scared.
Alone. She had one of those backpacks, you know with
the little spanish speaking girl on it. The girl
from the cartoon. I still have the theme song
stuck in my head. I told her it was going to be
okay. I kept saying that over and over. Lying. I told
her I had medicine and I could help her. I told
her I needed to give her a shot in the back of the
heck. She asked if it would hurt. I started
to cry. She hugged me. She said she
would be brave. She asked if I would take care

if her. That's exactly what I did. She turned
and I shot her in the back of her head. Just
like Lenny in that stupid book we had to read
in school. Does that make me good or bad?
I don't know anymore. everything 's upside down.

I opened her back pack and I found all these
notes and letters. This stuff 3 poisonous No one
in their right mind should read it. reading
this is like looking into the sun.

REMEMBER

~~WHEN COUGHING~~

~~COVER YOUR MOUTH~~

WER'E ALL DEAD

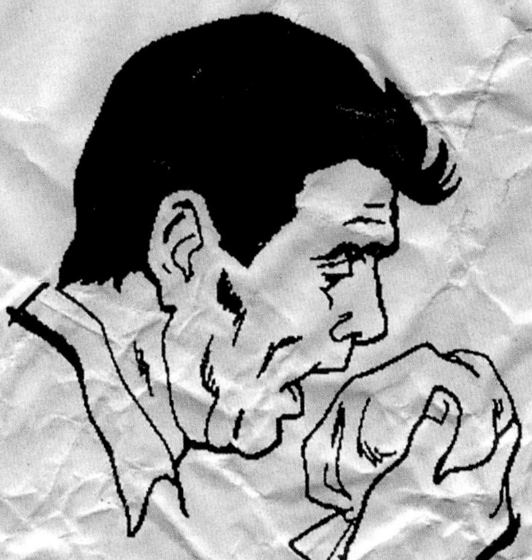

YOU CAN'T STOP THE
FLU FROM SPREADING

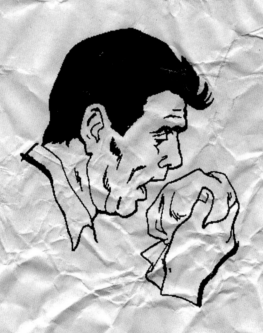

My Dearest —

I hope you are safe! The news is filled with stories of the flu and I wish you were here with us. The school closed, as a temporary measure so the children are driving me nuts! They can't understand why they can't go play with their friends.

The Anderson's down the street have the flu and there's a red X on the front door. Quarantine signs are posted all over town.

Remember Glen, the grocery store manager, well he told me several people have been shot for leaving quarantined homes! Can you believe this?

Kyle and Matt are fighting again — gotta run!

Love you!
Hurry home!

Me

A kid at
school bit
Jack — I'm
taking him
to the
doctor.

♡ dinner in fridge

Honey,

I woke up Early, couldn't sleep...
I Know that you feel that your going to be ok.
But the news about this new Flu-virus
has me Freaked out. You being a
CNA + Working with all those sick AND
OLD People... The CDC calls it a Pandemic!

Honestly, I'm afraid your going to
bring that shit home with you.
If not for us, then think about the Kids.

                    I Love you
P.S. - Watch the news!   Call me during lunch

Some Nutter in Frisco
Tried to Rob a BANK   XOXO
W/ FLU-BLOOD....
the WORLDS gone MAD.

I don't do
MORNINGS

Just got back from the
Doc. It's official, I
have the flu. Woohoo!
I'm upstairs sleeping
The baby's napping.

Mom,

Remember to

Get your FLU shot

@ the clinic - they

say it's Really bad

this year & I don't

want you to get

Sick! :(

Love you!

-K

MEMO

It's Hot outside already.
Look I'm begging you DON'T GO TO WORK!!
This THING is OFFICIALLY Scary NOW.
I need you here to help me. FOR REAL!
I'm Taking the Kids + going into Town for
Lumber and to see if I can get more
7.62 × 39 Ammo for the riffle.
Can you please fill the jugs I left out with water,
If we are dead-set on Staying put we have
to Secure the house, garage, + get supplies.
I know you don't have a permit to carry
your gun on you, but I'd feel safer if you did.
I'm leaving some cash, please go to the Store
and get as much canned meat + veggies as you can.
Also get: Bleach, distilled water, T.P., Candles, hell
Any thing you think we'll need! STAY CALM!
I'll BE BACK AROUND 5:00pm to Start BOARDING UP.
The NEWS SAYS there Are RIOTS IN All MAJOR CitiE
That's LESS THAN 3 HRS. From US!

July 8

The first case of this 'super flu' came to the UK this week, some guy in Scotland who was in the US on business; He has been quarentined THANK GOD

Shit across the pond looks bad, the whole country looks like it could fall, so much for being a superpower eh!

Dearest —

Please come home NOW! This place is going crazy. They wouldn't let me in the grocery store until I put on a surgical mask. Officer Morales had a shotgun pointed at this woman who's crime was SNEEZING! Can you believe that! I'm scared. The children and I need you here with us. Please leave San Fransisco and come home now!

The children are calling me — OMG! Johnny and his family next door have the flu. They just got quarantined! I was just there yesterday! OMG! What if I have it? What if I gave it to the children?

COME HOME NOW.
PLEASE!

Meg

August 13

Scotland is pretty bad right now, the border with England has been closed, but reports of new cases are already in London.

The boffins have created a cure so looks like this will all be over soon anyway.

Supplies of food and tea are pretty low in stores here, will take a run to the shops to stock up myself... just in case.

My Love —

Are you okay? I'm trying to hold things together but it's getting really hard. The mail has stopped and you don't answer your phone anymore.

The Anderson's house was torched. We could hear screams inside but no one would help. My God — Brother Doug held me back and said it was God's will! What kind of God condons murder and arsen? I will NOT go back there again and I don't care what you say.

Officer Morales came around with a dump truck collecting the dead. No services. Just a mass grave. The Stewart's behind us have three graves in the back yard.

Vickie is crying for you. I don't know what to tell her. I really can't do this alone!

I need you!

Me

Forget what anyone says. It takes a long time to turn. At least it did for Katie. She was bit and

...nt she was gonna be ok. Then she got s... ...was just like a flu at first. After about 5 days ...e started to forget stuff. Not just that though, ...e was acting weird. Like, really weird. I mean... ...a schizo, multi... per...

...her brain went in to overdrive and then s... ...elf. She wakes up one morning and she's o... ...them.

i'm getting really sick

Teresa wants to know how you are feeling today

whet is my dad?

Name: Tim   ID Number: 1193

RETURN TO THE DROP BOX LOCATED IN THE CAMP ST. TERESA CHILDREN'S WARD   Date:

Dear Doctor,

My dad is very sick. My mom sed I can't come out ov my room until he is o.k. I am scared. Please help my Daddy!

—Daniel

It's Brian. Get to the grocery store now and get as much non perishable food as you can. Then go to the hardware store and get the biggest containers you can. Fill them with water and gas.

WTF are you talking about. Where are you? Who's phone are you txting from?

I'm stationed at St. Teresa. It's a civilan's phone. Things are getting bad. Head to the cabin I will meet you.

When? I'm calling you.

Don't call! I can't talk.

You're freaking me out.

Good. Get as much ammo as you can. Leave for the cabin tonight. When you get there move everything upstairs. Board the windows and doors then destroy the staircase.

Why? How will you get in?

Bring a rope ladder. Don't let anyone in. If anyone tries to break in shoot them.

Jesus Brian WTF is going on.

Something is happening to the infected. They're attacking people.

You're serious?

Yes. Bring a bucket to piss and shit in. If this gets out it's over. The power will be out in two weeks. So will the water.

This doesn't make any sense.

Just trust me.

Ok. I'm going now. Will you be able to get out of there?

I think so.

137 cans of soup. 213 packs of Ramon. Some freeze dried shit. 53 packs of jerky. 24 boxes of cereal. I told them I was doing a food drive.

Good!

300 gallons of water and 50 gallons of gas. I can't fit any more.

893 rounds. I also got a couple of those wind up flash lights and radios and about 50 glow sticks. You owe me a lot of cash.

That's plenty for now.

Crow bar. Rope ladder. Chainsaw for stairs. Wood. Sledge hammer. Nails. Leaving for the cabin. When are you heading up?

Perfect. Good thinking. Don't worry about the money.

Don't hurt yourself! Take your time. I'm locked in at the moment. I'm waiting for the shit to hit the fan.

I'm at the cabin

Ok

Windows and doors boarded. Stairs gone. Pain in the ass.

I love you little brother.

I love you too. Everything ok?

Brian?

Please txt me.

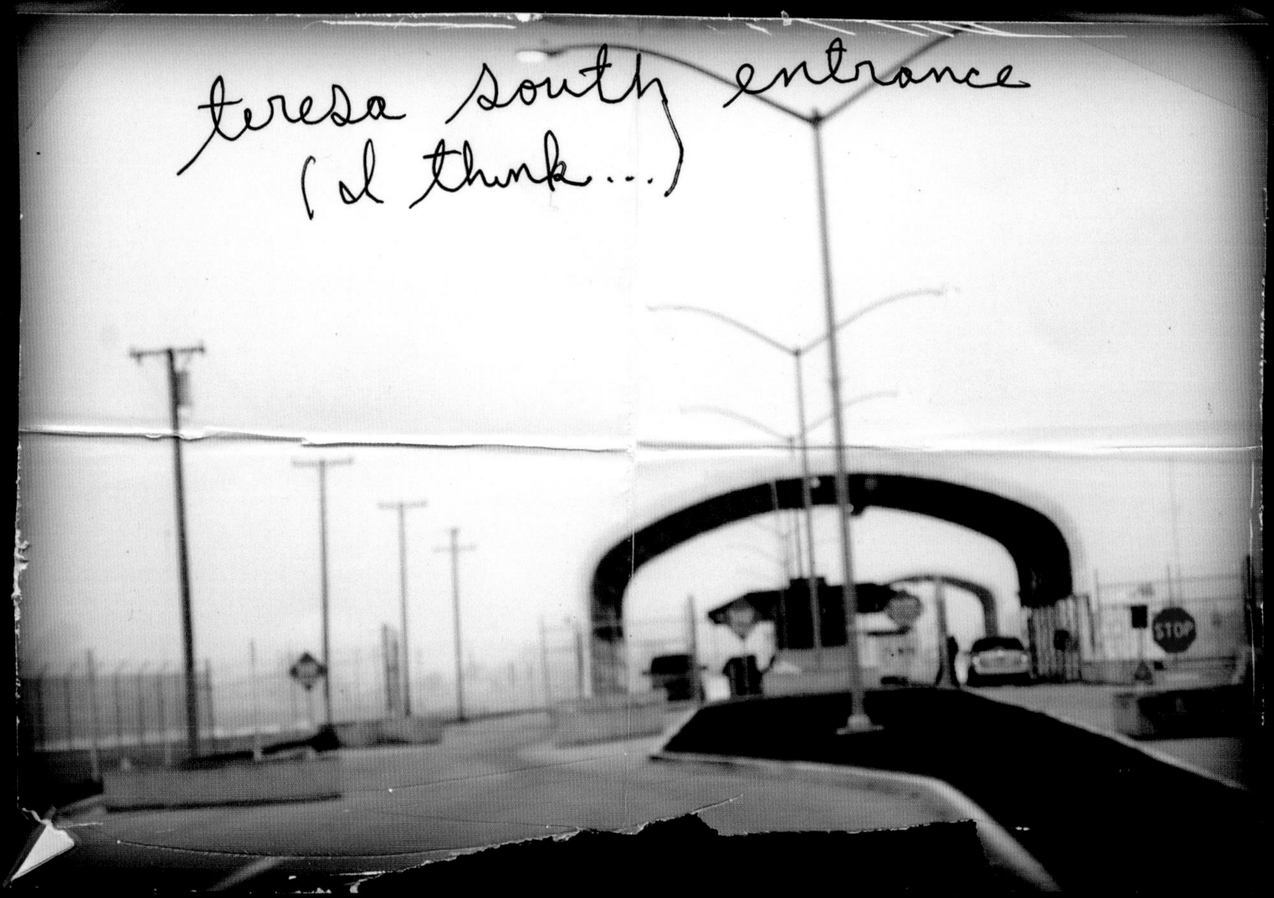
teresa south entrance
(I think...)
STOP

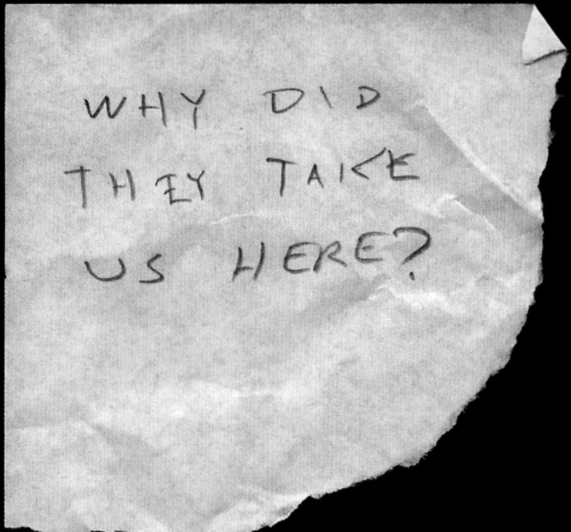
WHY DID
THEY TAKE
US HERE?

Doug, I sold the teresa passports. I know you think there will be a lot of hot girls there, but even if thats true theyll be sick. And Im sorry but I dont think condoms work against the flu.

Teresa wants to know how you are feeling today

Why are they biting each other?

Name: _____ ID Number: _____ Date: _____

I don't know if any of us are getting out of here. It's bad. They keep separating us. They say it's to keep the flu from mutating and spreading. There are rumors. There's an incinerator they burn the dead bodies in. People claim they've seen some of the really sick being taken in. I don't mean to scare you, but I guess if you actually get this I'm already gone. To be honest the incinerator st████████en the worst of it. There's a rumor ████████ of the sick are, Jesus I don't even kno████████rite this. They say that some of the sick a████g each other. The guys in charge are having trouble controlling the situation. There are protests. A guard shot a kid a few days ago. There was a suicide bombing, one of the sick made a homemade explosive and took out a few dozen people. Some of the sick have banded together. They call themselves THE TIME OF THE SEASON. They're planning to do something. I don't know how bad thing████ are on the outside. No ████

away from Teresa. I know we never had a real relationship. I don't know how or why things got the way they did. I'm sorry. Not sure if it means anything. In hindsight I would have done things a lot differently. I guess that's life, one big clich█ love you. Me.

LyDia LUNDy

CAMP TeResA
IS FuckeD!

Ashley + I Are
HeADing NORTH
To THE CABIN
In VictoRiA.
   I Love you.
     JOn

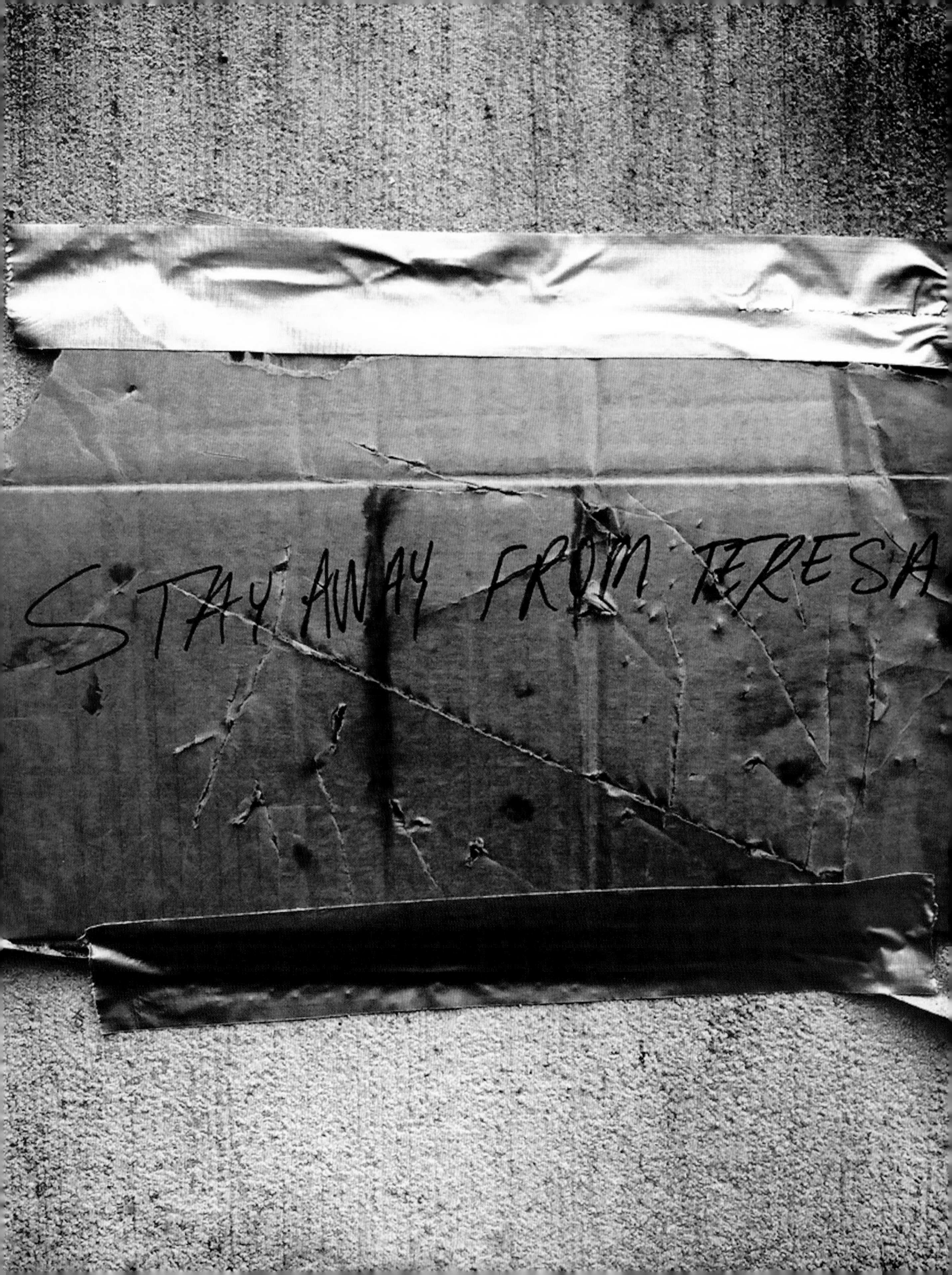
STAY AWAY FROM TERESA

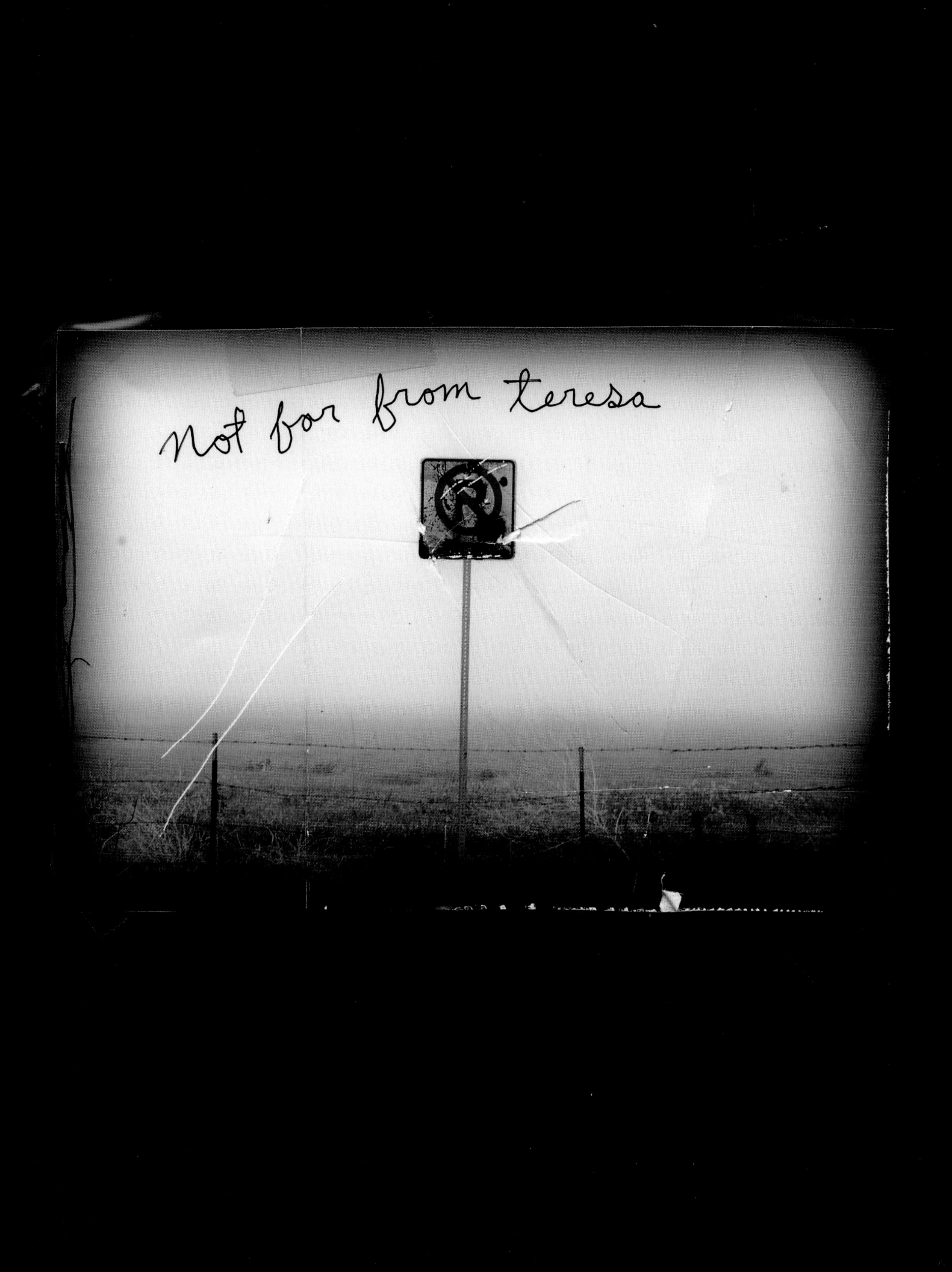
not far from teresa

KEEP
QUIET
THEYRE
HERE

We saw a man bite a
ladys face, we ran with
mommy then there lots of
people biting each other.
I'm afraid.

olives
lettuce
4 toms (roma)
1 yellow onion
2 red bell peppers
celery
1 1/2 cups green lentils
fresh parsely
fresh thyme
cilantro
bread
goat cheese
2 sweet potatoes
veg. stock
garlic powder
sesame seeds
beer

PLEASE READ

Have you seen my baby? His tag
says Daniel but he is not Daniel

Heading back to the Camp to look again

DO NOT GO IN

REPEAT DO NOT SEEK SHELTER AT ST. TERESA

I will be back through this area
Please post if any news
I hear there is unrest and people may be
smuggled out by sympathetic staff
PRAY THIS IS TRUE
Seek your loved ones at the broken perimeters
but DO NOT SEND YOUR CHILDREN IN

My baby looks like this:

PLEASE POST - HE MIGHT BE OUT HERE
name is Eliza G

DON'T LET
THEM BITE
YOU

The best is yet to come.

congratulations on your graduation

the dogs won't
go near them

even the ones
who were bit
but aren't zombies
yet
the dogs know

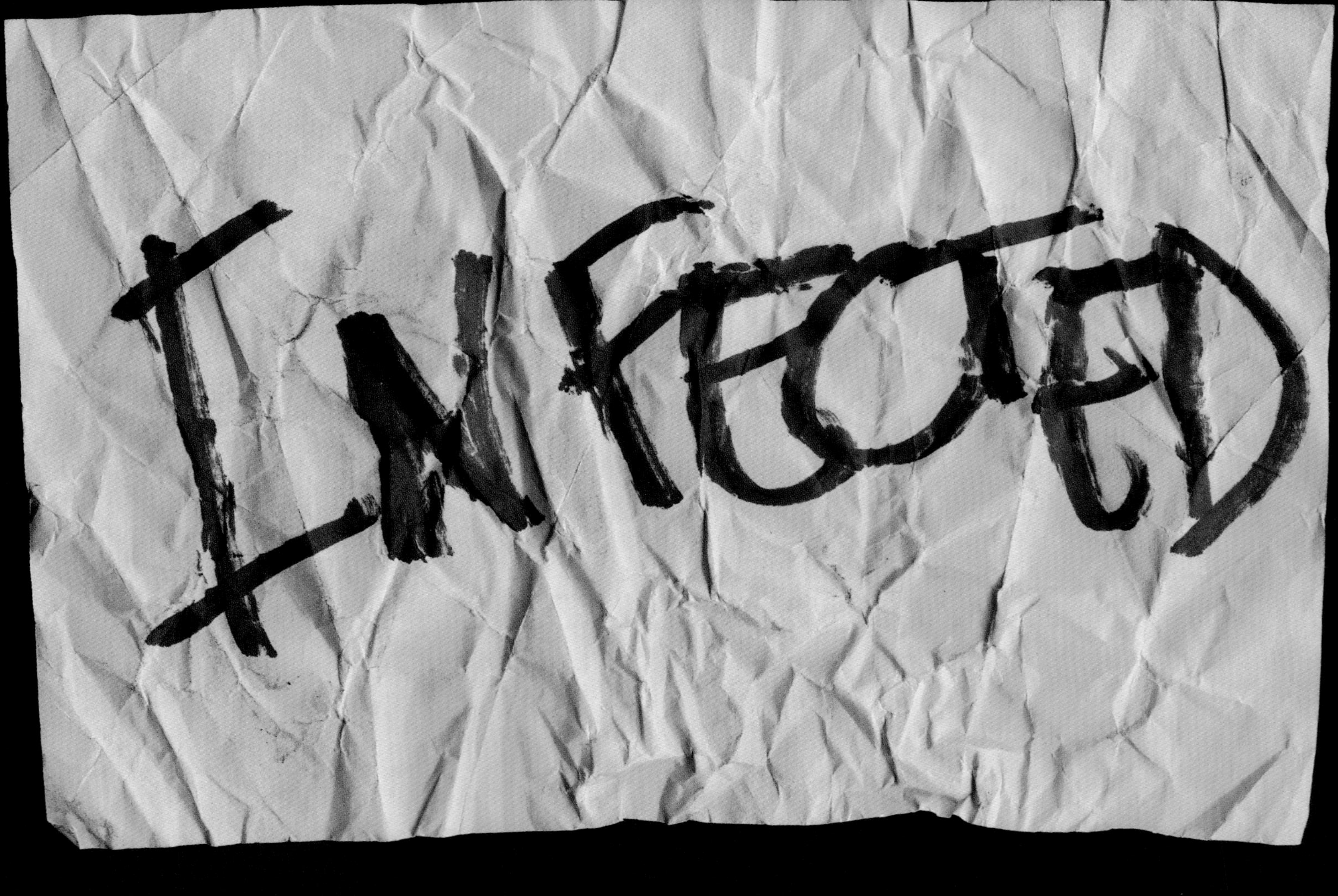
INFECTED

don't be
alarmed,
there's one
in your car.
Text me

We're heading to

Atlanta to the CDC

MayBe its all just
a hoax or something??

IF YOU
GET THIS
JACK IS DEAD
SORRY ABOUT
YOUR COUCH.

ZOMBIE
LEFT
OVERS

(JACK)

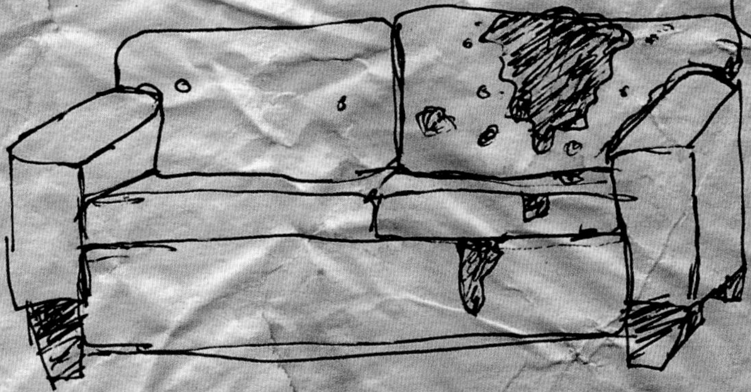

Mom.

MOTHER FUCKING ZOMBIES
ARE REAL!

-K

The baby turned. I'm
sorry. Its all my fault.
I shouldn't have left her
in the car.

...up in a convenience store with a mother and her two children. Mary the mother had lost her husband to what they thought were robbers. A courageous man. Anyway, it didn't take long for them to find us. They were banging on the windows the next day. Within hours there were dozens of them. When they broke through I tried to fight them off. I knew I wouldn't survive so I ran. I ran and left them. They were able to maneuver the horde, and I ended... but they... I can't look at myself anymore.

R BITE

I WAS BIT HERE. IS THAT OK?!

- GET SHOT GUN FROM NEXT DOOR
- SET FIRE TO FRANK'S HOUSE
- CUT BANK MANAGER'S THROAT
- SET EX-WIFE ON FIRE
- SHOOT SMART MOUTH KID ACROSS STRE
- TAKE THAT HARLEY DAVIDSON FROM FRAN
- POKER WITH THE GUYS
- ASK EMMA OUT ON THAT DATE
- CHAINSAW FUEL
- GET A CHAINSAW

FUCK YOU FRANK

KILL FRANK

FRANK ISN'T BETTER THAN ME

TO WHOM IT MAY CONCERN

IN THE EVENT THAT I AM BITTEN BY A
ZOMBIE . . . .

TIE ME DOWN AND PUT YOUR BOOT
THROUGH MY FACE, BECAUSE I AM
COMING BACK TO RIP THE EYEBALLS OUT
OF EVERY SINGLE ONE OF YOU SELFISH
FUCKS WHO ARE LEFT ON THIS PATHETIC
PLANET

YOU CALL PULLING A GUN OVER A
BOTTLE OF WATER OR TIN OF DOG FOOD
'SURVIVING' . . . . WELL TRY SURVIVING
WITHOUT YOUR FUCKING EYES

I WAS
BIT.
DO NOT
ENTER.

CHRIS

LAUREN

KATY

DAN

JACOB

SARAH

I BULLET LEFT

they killed a
bunch of infected kids
at the school. People got
upset. There was a fight
and some people got shot.
I decided to leave.

I ~~think~~ think it
was probably the right
thing to do with
the kids. thats why
I'm leaving. I want
to be alone so I don't
have to kill kids.
also tom keeps throwing
things at my balls.

JULIE

IM NOT DEAD

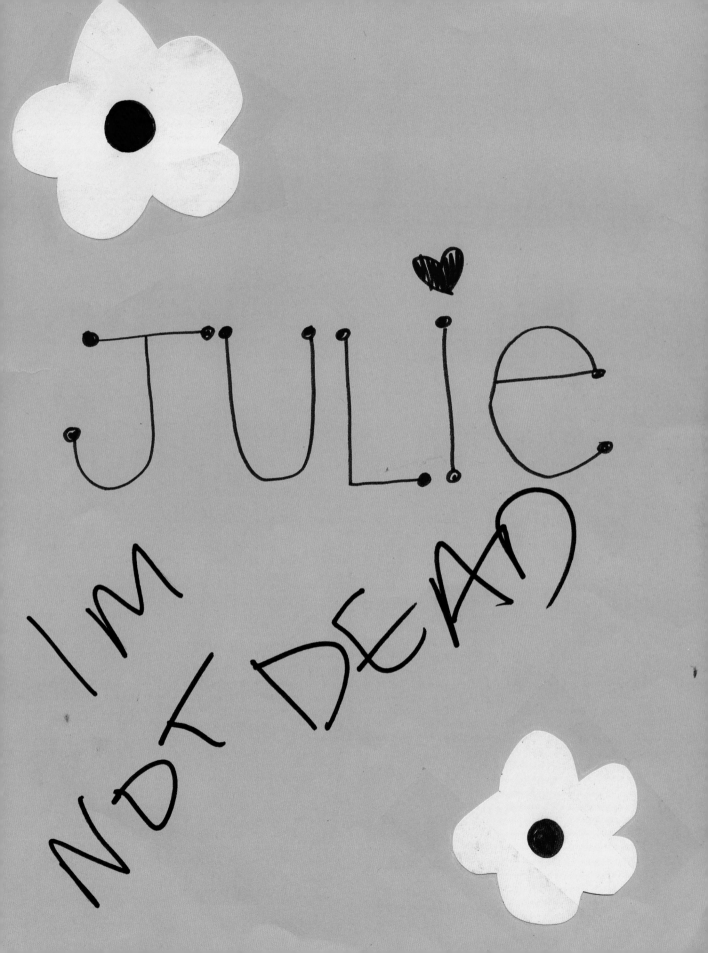

HELP

Fuck You!

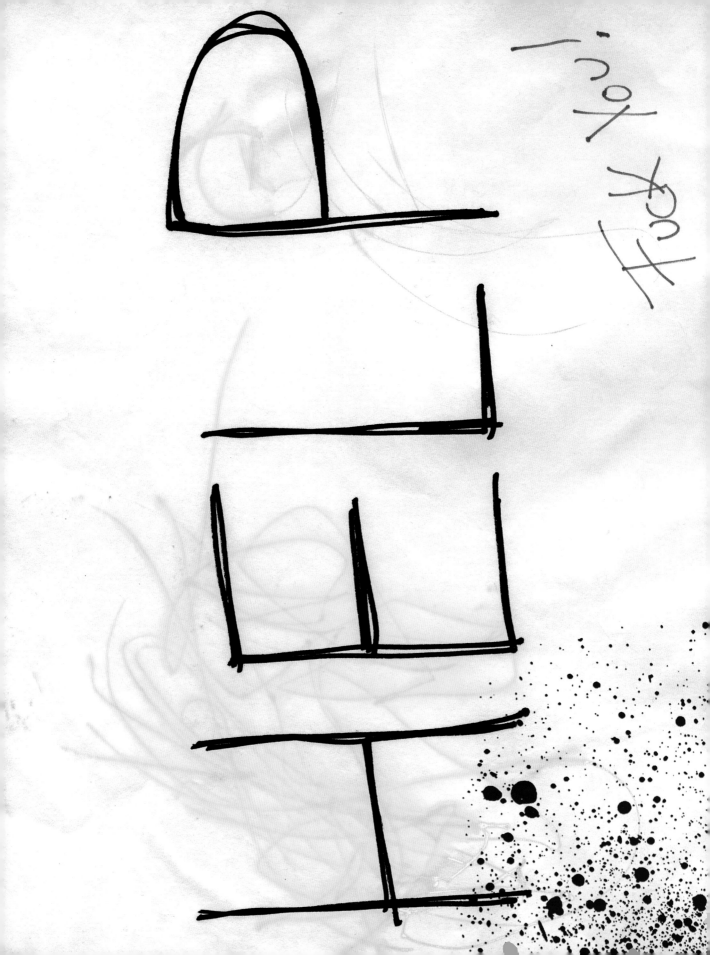

they weren't
bitten, I just told
you that so it
would be eaisier
for you to leave them.

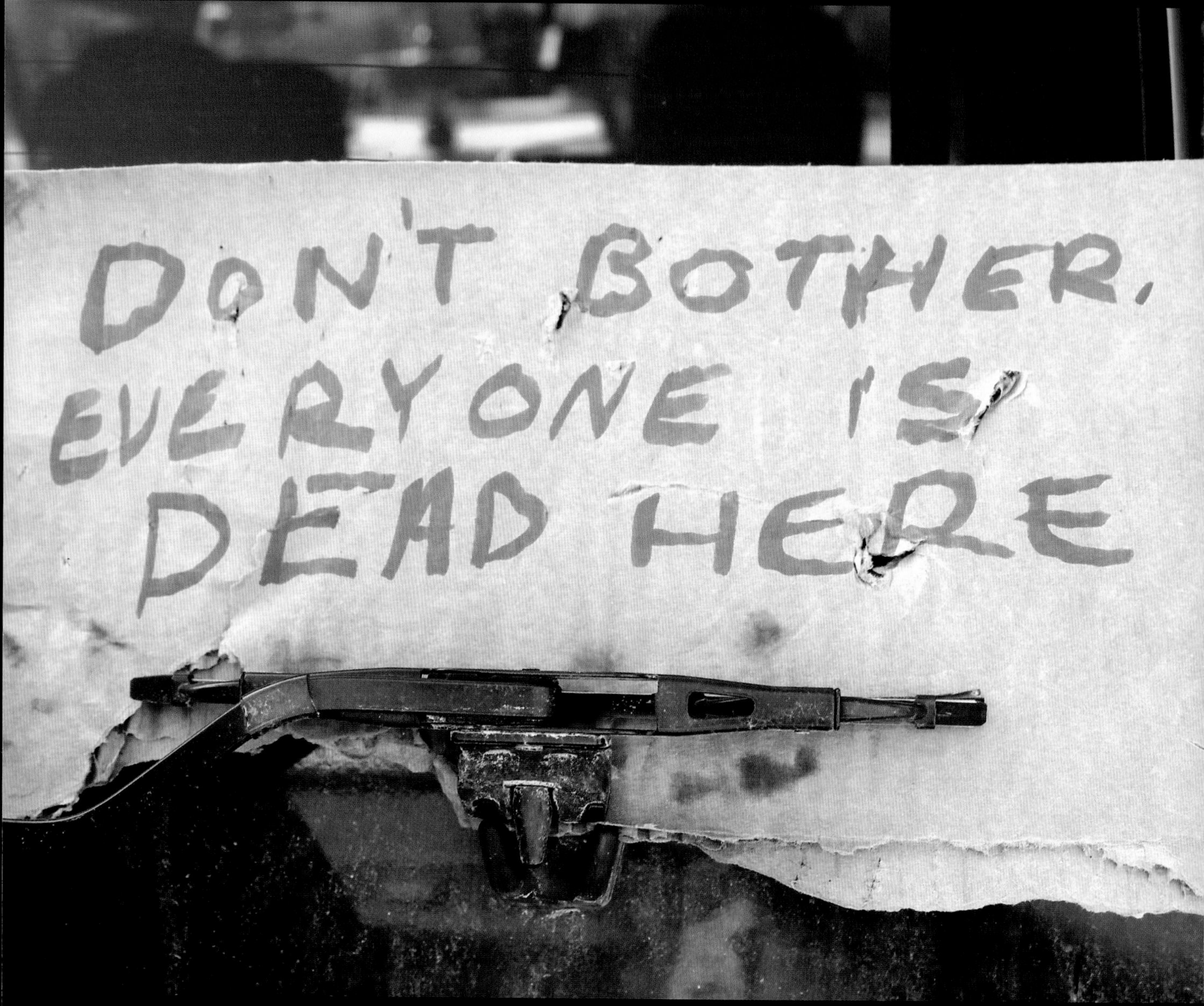
DON'T BOTHER.
EVERYONE IS
DEAD HERE

In the event that I am bitten, please don't hesitate. Do not feel as though you owe me anything. I am not your wife. I am not their mother. I am the problem and for their sake you have to deal with me. Please don't let the children see me at the end if you can avoid it. I don't want them to remember me that way.

Please make it quick. I don't want you to suffer any more than you already have in watching this happen to me. This isn't your fault. If I am still coherent and capable, just leave me the gun and I will do it myself. Please my love, I don't want to hurt anyone, especially you.

Do you remember the day we spoke about what I wanted if I ever became seriously ill and there was no hope of recovery? Remember your promise that day and always remember that I love you. Know that I would do the same for you because in the end what happens to us isn't important. Our first responsibility is to our children. Keep them safe, and keep me in their hearts, and yours.

I Love You,
Rebecca

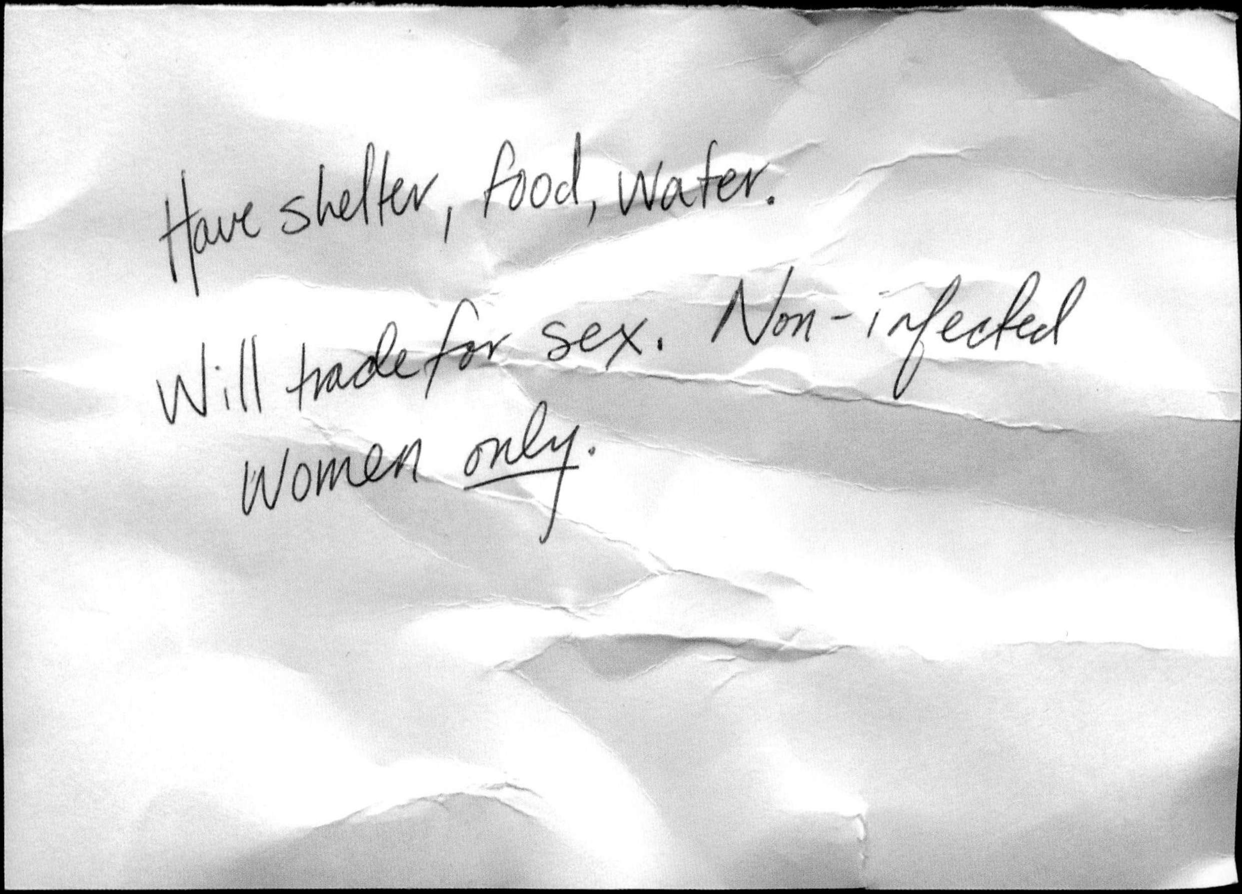
Have shelter, food, water.

Will trade for sex. Non-infected women <u>only</u>.

There r three
of them inside.
if you kill one
take a tab.

things
got
bad

2 3 4 5

this is what he used

dead inside

and, I had to tell someone. I cannot explain it but, you need to understand what I am doing. The choice not to kill her is my own! She is was my wife and, no matter what she has become, I still love her. Though I've had to chain her in the garage in recent days I refuse to break my marriage vows! Sleep has become a precious commodity as Helen screams constantly. I must find a cure. There must be a cure? I will continue to test the vaccine on those I've captured in the hope

Whoever finds this, I was not infected. I took my own life. My 2 year old daughter and I were in the car. We needed supplies so we went to the grocery. I locked her in the car and went into the store. When I came out the car was surrounded by them. It was over a 100 degrees outside. I tried for hours to lure them away. My little girl died from the heat, surrounded by monsters. I could hear her crying for me. I can't stop thinking about her suffering. I'm sorry. I hope I'm going to see her again.

FUCK. THE CHRISTIANS WERE RIGHT!

all my ~~[scribbled out]~~ life
I've been afraid of dying.
Now that ~~[scribbled out]~~ it's in front of me
I'm not. I'm actually happy.

The vegas strip is barricaded. They won't let us out of the hotel. Earlier in the casino things got out of control. People wanted to leave but the doors were blocked. There were soldiers with guns telling us that we are being quarantined. One guy got really upset and upended a black jack table. Chips went flying everywhere and suddenly no one cared about getting out they all just went for the chips. There were too many of them. The dealers and pit bosses just watched. It didn't take long for the things to get out of control. After sacking the the black jack tables a couple of guys grabbed the table and used it as a ramrod to break through the casino doors. The guards, they didn't even give a warning, they just opened fire. It was the most horrible thing I'd ever seen, up until about 30 minutes later when the infected from St. Teresa showed up. There were thousands of them.

This is not a conspiracy
or a prophecy. People want
it to mean something
it doesn't — it's how
we became extinct
that's it

WE DID
THIS

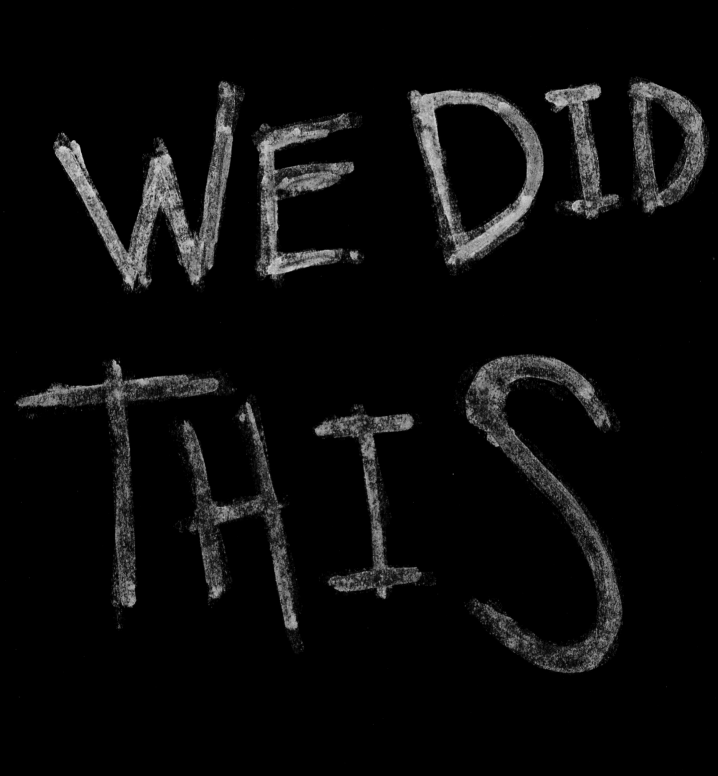

KILL

US

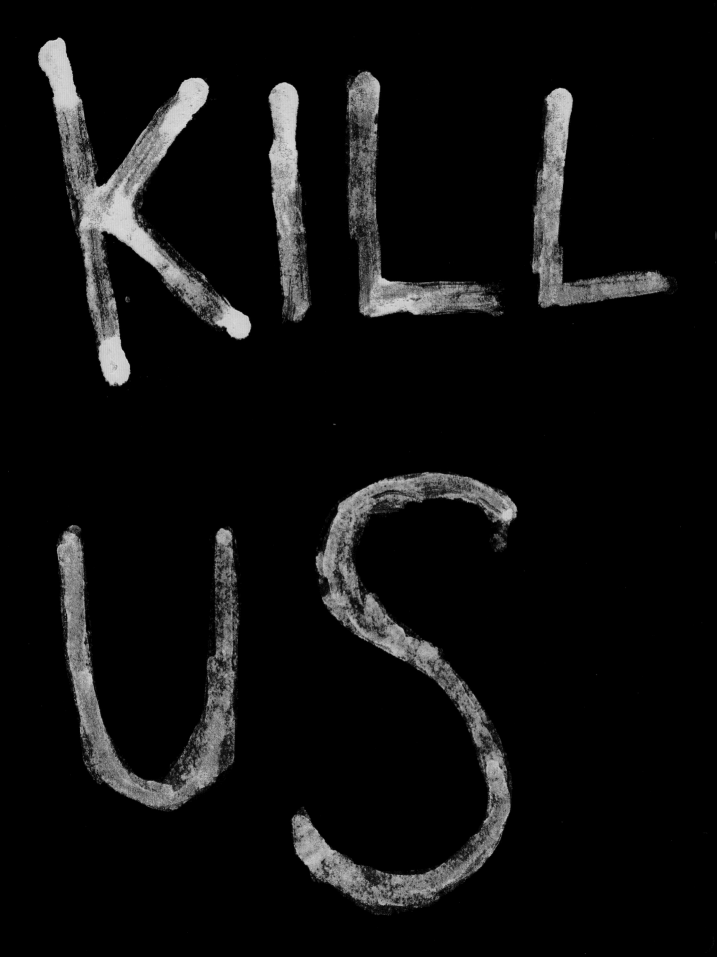

Dear Jenny,

I don't know that you will ever see this or that I will ever see you again. It was a mistake to send you on ahead. We should have stood together. There's only two of us left now. The other six died or ran off back near Calumet City. Brian, the other fella with me got banged up real bad. We're sitting in this old truck stop down by the West Virginia border. I hope you found your Momma and I hope someday I find you. I can hear them outside now, they sound hungry. I best go help Brian he looks sick.

I love you
Thomas

Alex,
we've gone
north where's
there's supposed
to be lots of them.
we hope to meet
up with you again
soon.
-Jess

To whoever finds this,
    There's a gun and some supplies
under the counter. I won't be needing
them anymore. Hope you have
better luck than I did.

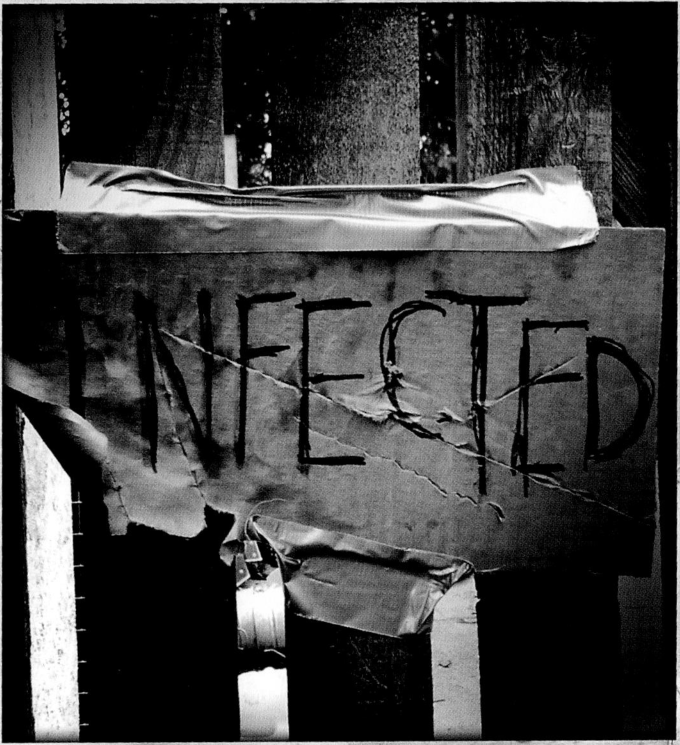
INFECTED

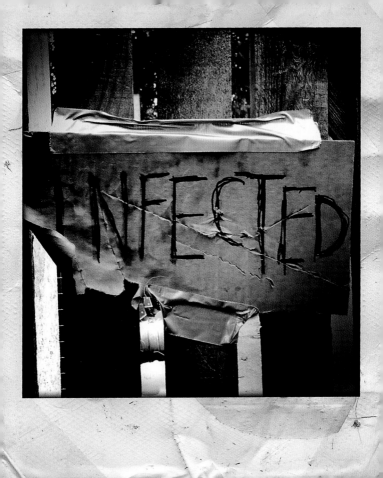

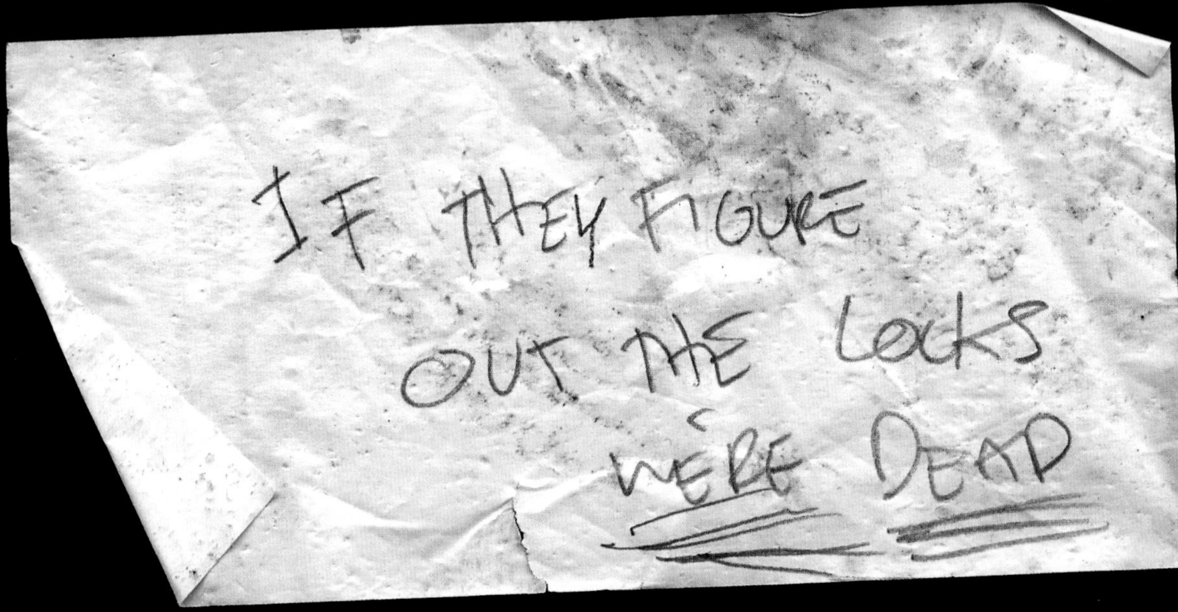
IF THEY FIGURE
OUT THE LOCKS
WE'RE DEAD

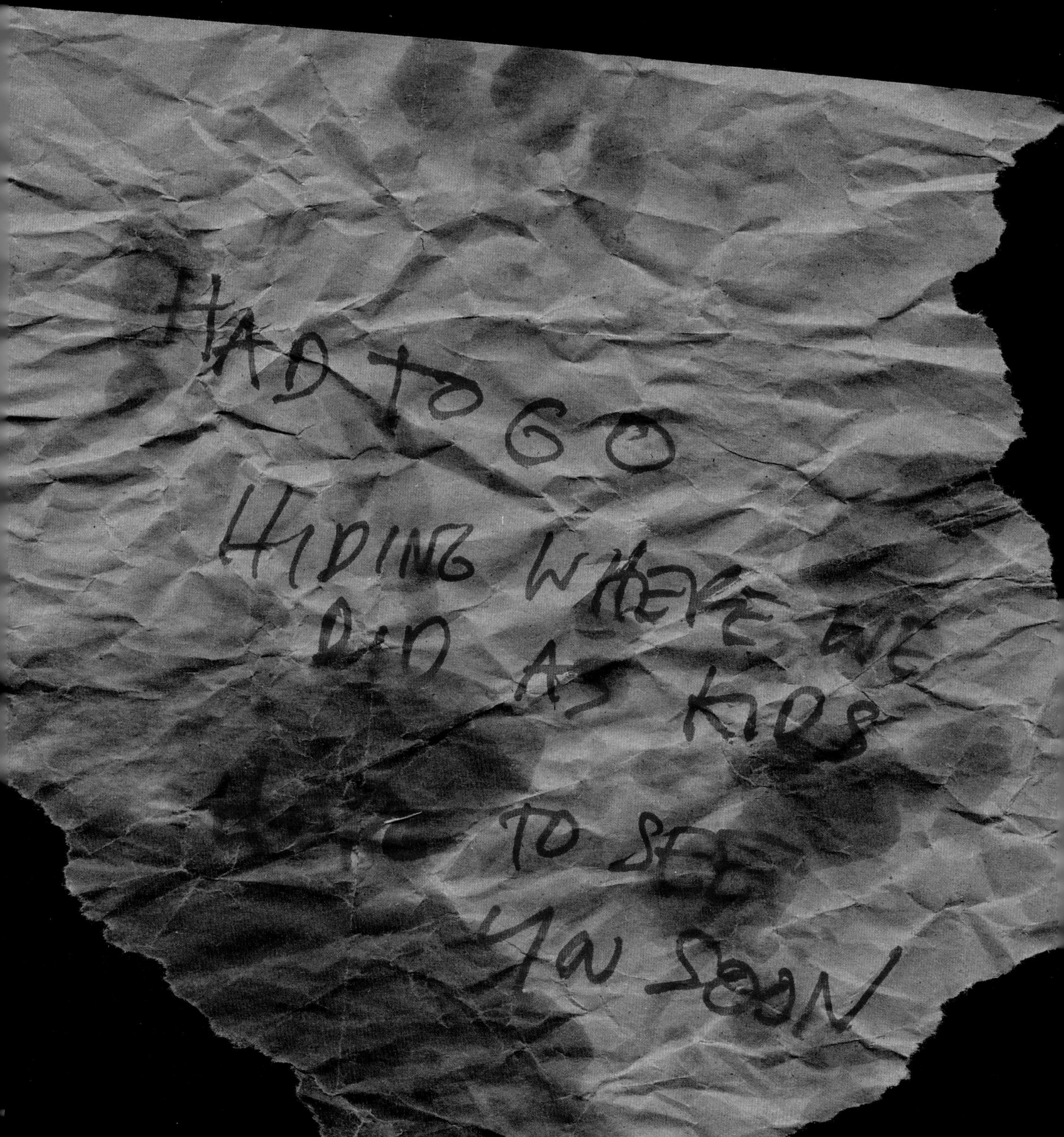
HAD TO GO
HIDING WHERE WE
DID AS KIDS
TO SEE
YOU SOON

To whom it may concern,

In the case I get bit by a zombie...

Fuck it.

I did get bit. I'm in the basement.

If you are in MY HOUSE raiding MY SUPPLIES you had better fucking kill me you asshole.

Here, I'll save you a bullet,

Use this sledgehammer.

Thanks.

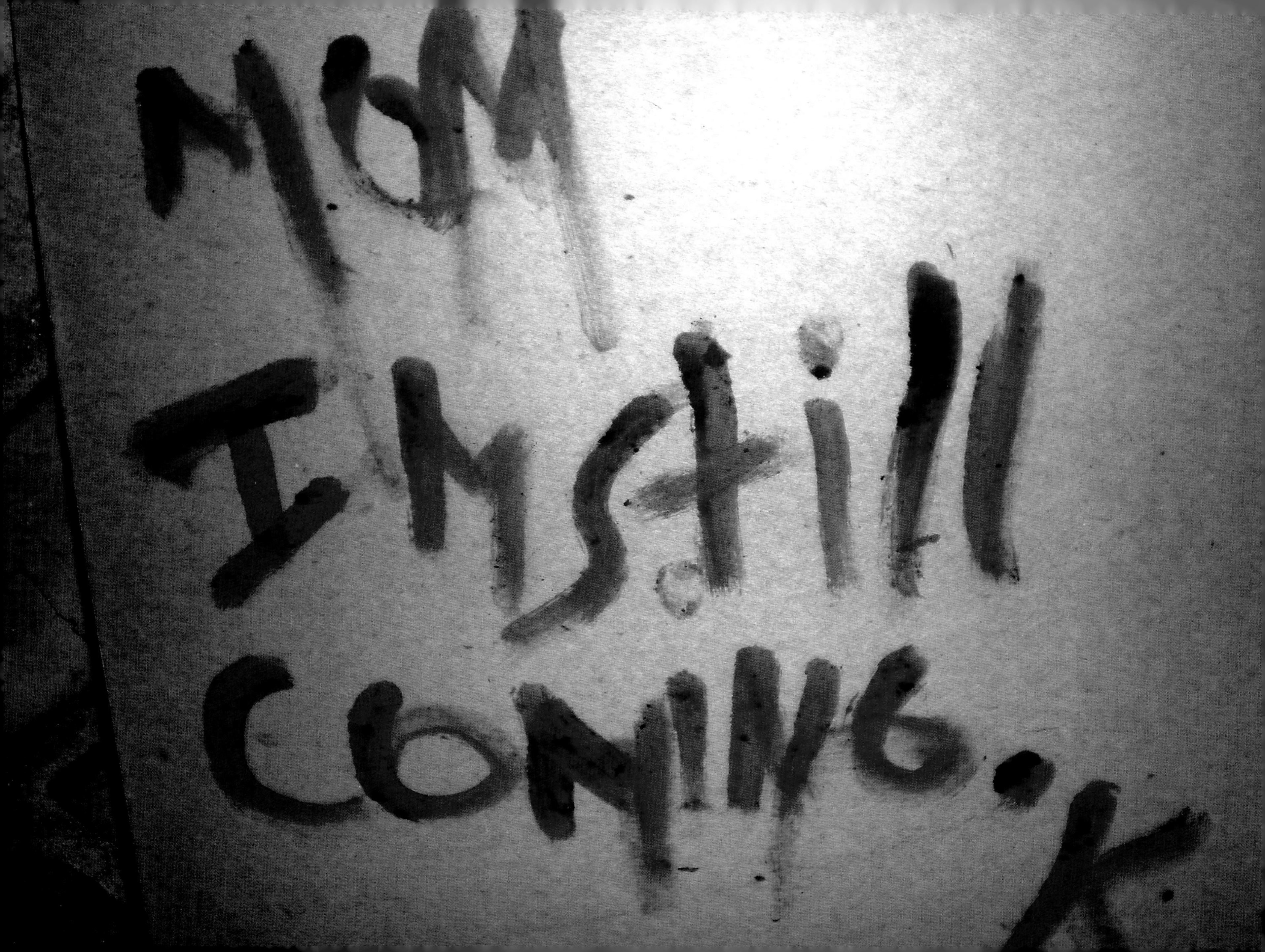
MOM
I'M still
COMING. x

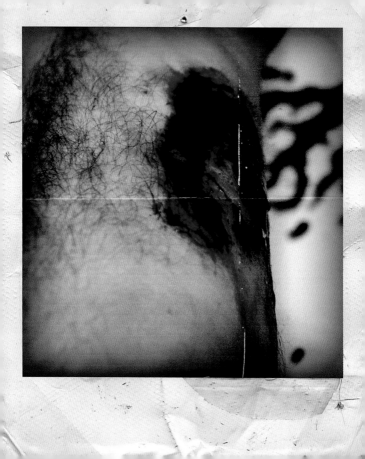

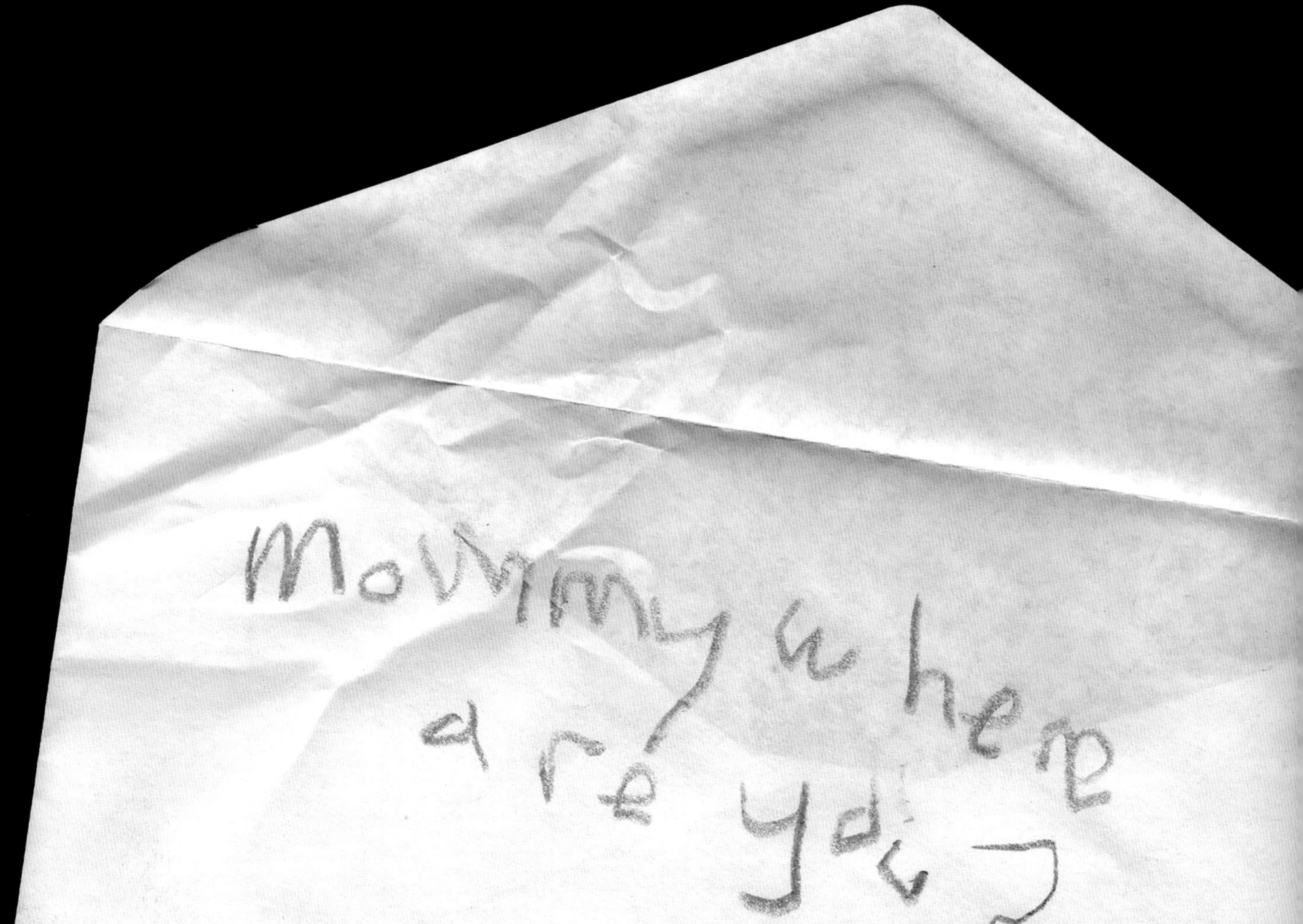
mommy where
are you?

Don't tell
the others, but I'm
sorta happy all this
happened

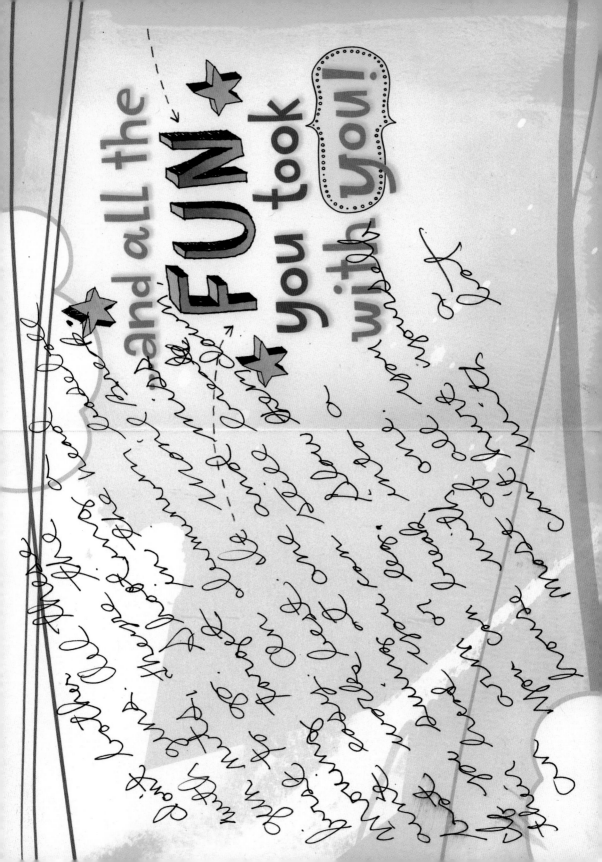

...and all the **FUN** you took with you!

the helicopter was
heading in the same
direction we are.
Maybe the base is safe

Lots of maybes

You wake up in a hospital. But a special kind of hospital. They call it Crisis Stabilization. A doctor tells you that you've suffered a trauma. He says you have what's called a dissociative fugue. Only that doesn't really capture what you're experiencing. You don't know who you are. You don't know where you are. You don't even really know what you are. Some of the words the doctor uses you know, most you don't. He tells you that everything is going to be okay. In hindsight he is very very wrong. Things are not going to be okay. The crisis is not going to be stabilized.

It's October, the shit hasn't completely fallen apart at St. Teresa. Slowly you start to remember. You remember everything up to the testing facility. You remember that getting paid 30k to test flu vaccines seemed like a sweet deal. You tell the doctor what you remember and the the serious man shows up. There are tests, lots of them.

The serious man asks lots of questions. He asks if you know what's in your stomach. The question seems odd and you wonder if your brain is misfiring. He asks again. Is this a riddle?

You don't know what's in your stomach. They make you shit into plastic containers, the same kind your mom used to put left overs in. You're taken to St. teresa. Then you wake up in Barstow California. Another dissociative fugue. It's like time traveling. It's late November. What ever happened at teresa is a mystery to you. In god forsaken Barstow, where the Golden State shits itself into the desert, people are eating each other.

Has it always been this way?

Mom and I made it out of North Carolina. IT's like we have been walking forever. We lost Daddy. He died trying to get us past one of the checkpoints. They were all over our car. Most of them used to be soldiers. I don't know where we are right now. IT's some restaurant. We pushed stuff up against the door. I don't think there's any of them out there now. I hope not. Mom's asleep, it's dark and I am scared. I said a prayer for my daddy. If you are reading this maybe you could too.

My name is Tara and I am 12.
We were from Camp Lejeune. My Daddy was a Marine.

I never loved you
and I'm glad you are
now one of them.

You should
have gone
to chuch

I left him full o...

"Don't worry, I'll be...

I took only some...

this Baseball Bat. t...

hand grenades, and Any...

Fair you could say.

That bastard fucked my wife in J...

He shot her head right in front...

She had to be mine... my love...

and HE splattered my dreams...

beautiful brains on the...

So NOW...

th...

Date Unsure

I'm writing this to apologize

to the young girl I shot. I'm very sorry

I was scared for my life, but thats no excuss.

please forgive me,

Sorry Forever

things you should
know

1. Sometimes they
turn before they
die. Watch out, those
ones are fast..

2. Sometimes they
turn after they die,
those ones are slow

3. If you see doug,
tell him i'm looking
for him

i'm fine.

great argument.

and be mature.

I got it. I thought I was

Meet at my house.

I resent the ~~Fact~~
that you are
MAKING <u>Me</u> apologize for
something I DIDN'T Do. Besides
a STUPID EARTHQUAKE KIT isn't going
to <u>DO ANYTHING</u> AGAINST THESE

THINGS. AND you SHOULD Know
that I know ABOUT you AND Chuck.

Let's not argue anymore
about what weapon is best
If you want to carry around
that Chainsaw that's your
business. All i was saying
is that between the gas
and the horse it seems more
trouble than It's worth.
Like Bill.

Leaving California. Heading north. This place is fucked. Here's to a white xmas. I hope these fuckers freeze.

Dear Reader,

This document is meant to account my ordeals throughout this atrocity. I hope by reading this you may gain a better understanding of this... my... possibly even your situation. I will write everything down to the best of my knowledge. I apologize for any inconsistand...

doug, went
to look for
duct tape
with the
crazy ass-
hole.

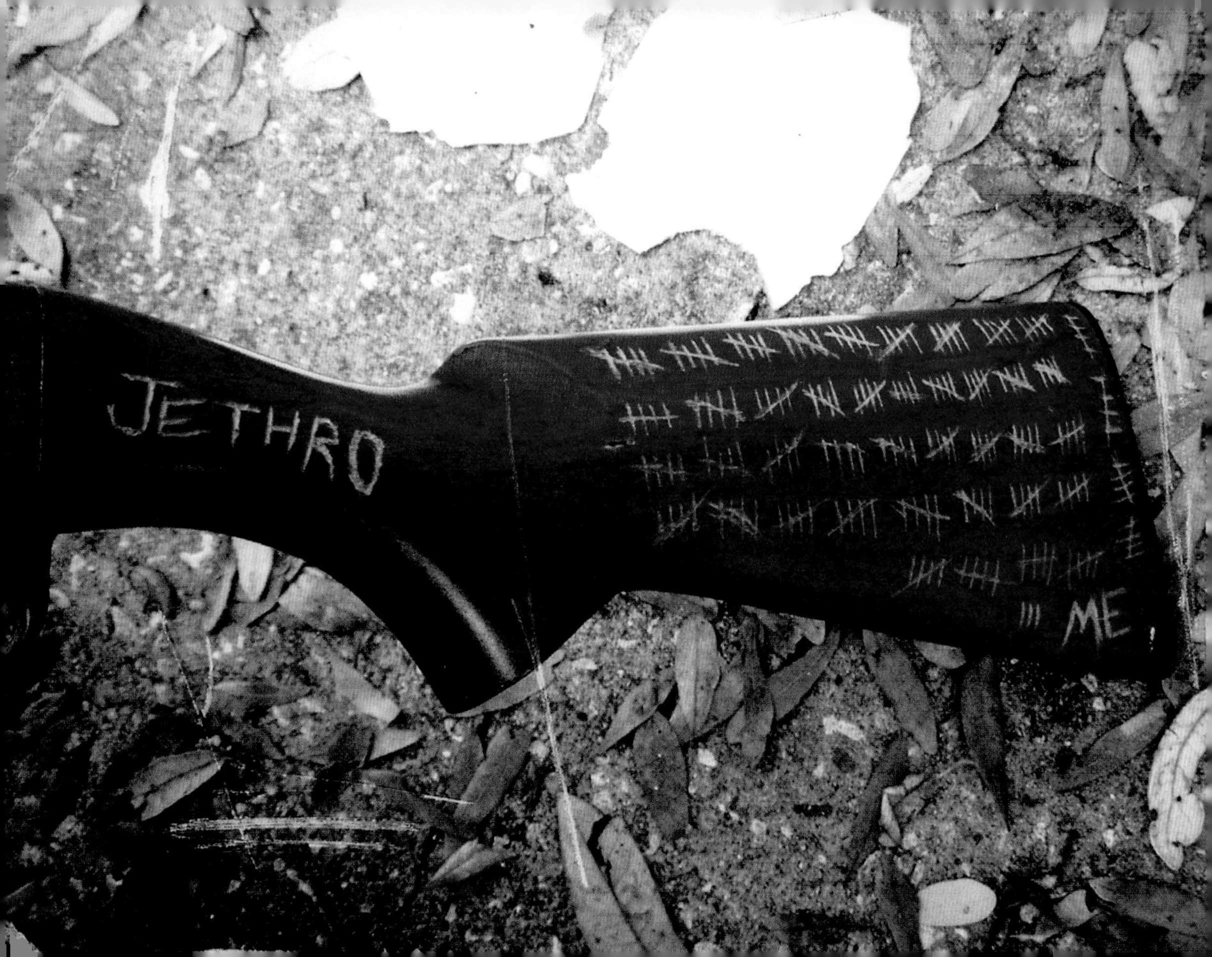
JETHRO
ME

I'm only 15 I just wanted
to have a normal life. I'm
pretty sure I'll never have sex
now. I should have let
Danny have sex with me when
I had the chance. This is all
So useless. Mom won't stop
praying she says that that's all
we have left. I still want to
Survive though I don't want
to end up like that
little girl they found by the river

I abandoned my family. I screwed them over - told them I'd be back in a bit - and never came through. We were low on food. I said I'd go scavenge, but I packed up my supplies and left. And I didn't just take ~~my~~ *my* supplies, I took ~~everybodys~~ EVERYBODY'S

...they waited too. They kept waiting. I went back a few days ago. Nothing but a bloody mess. I left them unarmed and starving...

- Mara

I saw this
coming. Not the
zombie thing, but
the end of the
world

MISSING
REWARD

DENT

BASEBALL BAT

I KILLED 6 OF THEM
WITH THIS. IT'S GOOD
LUCK. I LOST IT
ON MAPLE $ LINCON.

1. Go to the bathroom. You never know when the next rest stop will be.

2. Clean underwear! Mama always said if I don't change my undies, bad things will happen.

3. Turn off the stove.

4. Don't forget to bring a towel!

5. Wear shoes suitable for running.

6. Wear long sleeves! Don't want infected blood directy on the skin.

7. Bring cricket bat. Multifunctional. Weapon? Crutch? Splint? All of the above!

8. Save the dog! Dog can kill zombies, can't they? I hope so.

9. Watch your back at all times.

10. Wear sunscreen.

We lit them on fire, the
safe house is gone.

Lisa was inside

So was the food

CLOSED ZOMBIES

are you fucking kidding me? Warning about zombies in comic sans!

What is wrong with comic sans?

I BLAME ALL OF THIS ON COMIC SANS

I was bit.

I've been on the run for months, doing whatever it takes to survive. I have put a bullet in everyone I've ever loved. I killed my parents and then my boyfriend. ~~Because I don't~~ Some day I think I'd be better off if I killed myself. But I go on fighting and killing.

do you think it's as BAD as DENMARK?

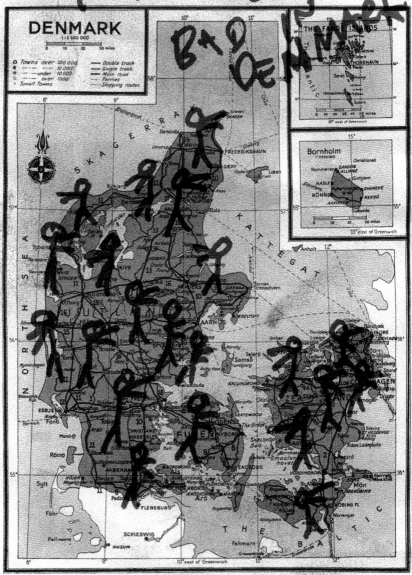

DENMARK

probably

15

Decided to Board
up the windows in
the basement. Not
a good choice.

One crawled in
through the
window.

Bye Dad

I killed ~~too.~~ I invited him in and killed him. He had the guns, the, Ammo, And an aditude. He would never stop Arguing with my father, Always mouthed off. I invited him in because he was smart. I never thought he'd be too smart. He hit dad.
My dad, our boss man with the plan. ~~too~~ had good ideas, but it had to be his way, Always. We were friends before this. I knew he would be difficult, but I thought he'd fall in. I took him out back And strangled him. Cant waste bullets. He knew I was doing it, And probably knew why. After that I stripped him and hung him off ~~the lot.~~ for bait. His dog really misses him.

WE NEED TO
TALK!

BRING YOUR
RADIO & BREAD

— DAVE

**BEM-VINDO
AOS
ESTADOS UNIDOS**

DEPARTAMENTO DO TESOURO
ALFÂNDEGA DOS ESTADOS UNIDOS

DECLARAÇÃO ALFANDEGÁRIA

19 CFR 122.27, 148.12,

egar, cada viajante ou chefe de família deverá prestar as seguintes informações (somente UMA
ração escrita por família é exigida):

renome

ome

3. Inicial do Segun-
do Nome

4. Data do Nascimento
(dia/mês/ano)

panhia Aérea/Nome do Veículo ou Nome do Navio ou No. da Placa do Veículo

6. Número de
Familiares
Acompanhantes

aís de Cidadania

7. (b) País de Residência

Endereço nos E.U.A. (Número e Rua/Hotel/Endereço para correspondência nos E.U.A.)

ndereço nos E.U.A. (Cidade)

8. (c) Endereço nos E.U.A. (Estado)

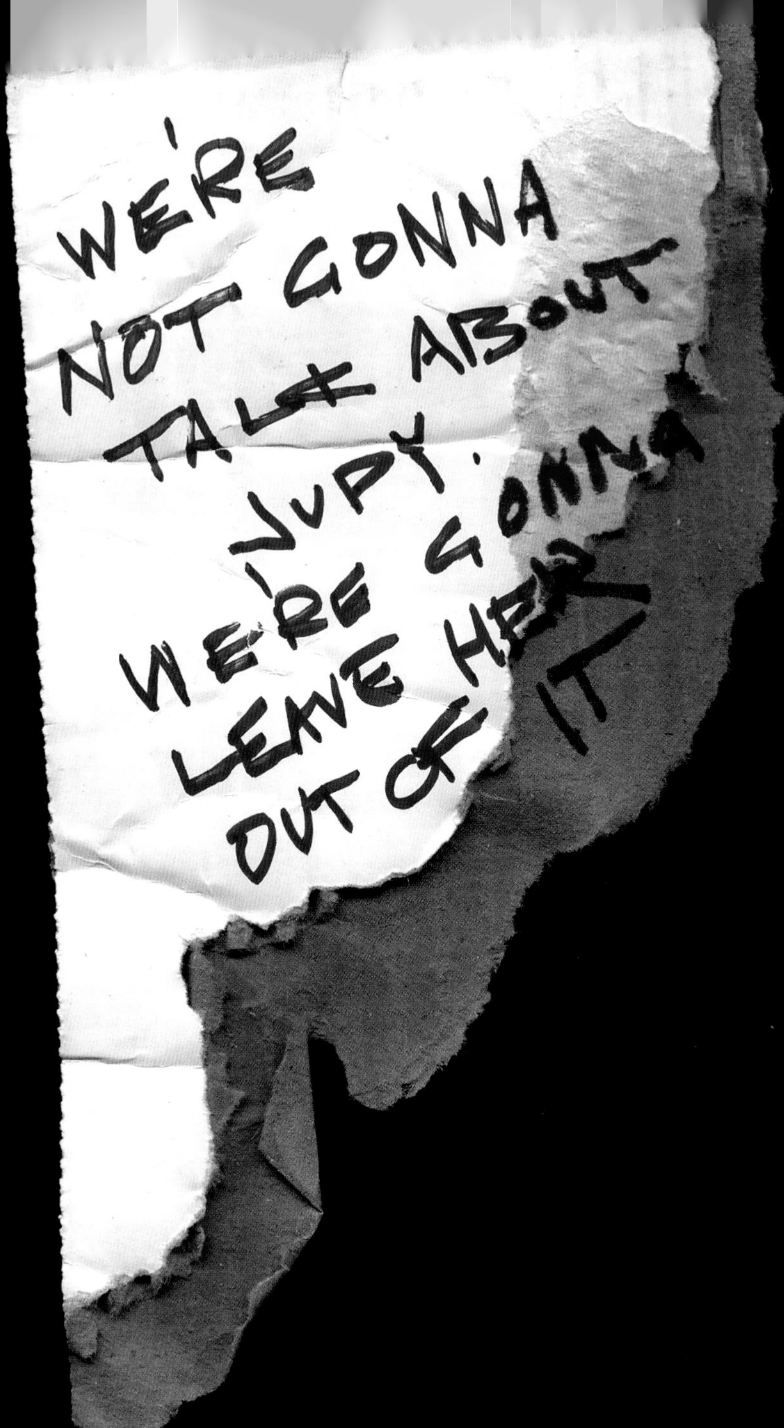
WE'RE
NOT GONNA
TALK ABOUT
JUDY.
WE'RE GONNA
LEAVE HER
OUT OF
IT

im hiding in
the attic you fuckers.
if you could read you
could get my ass.

Most people when asked would say that the most terrible thing that has ever happend to them would be the death of a loved one. Mine is something I did. You see, all of my loved-ones had already died before the start of this whole... terrible thing. I found the bodys of some, some were just missing, and one, died in my arms. I thought there was nothing worse. I was so very wrong.

i miss the Internet.

really just porn
i think

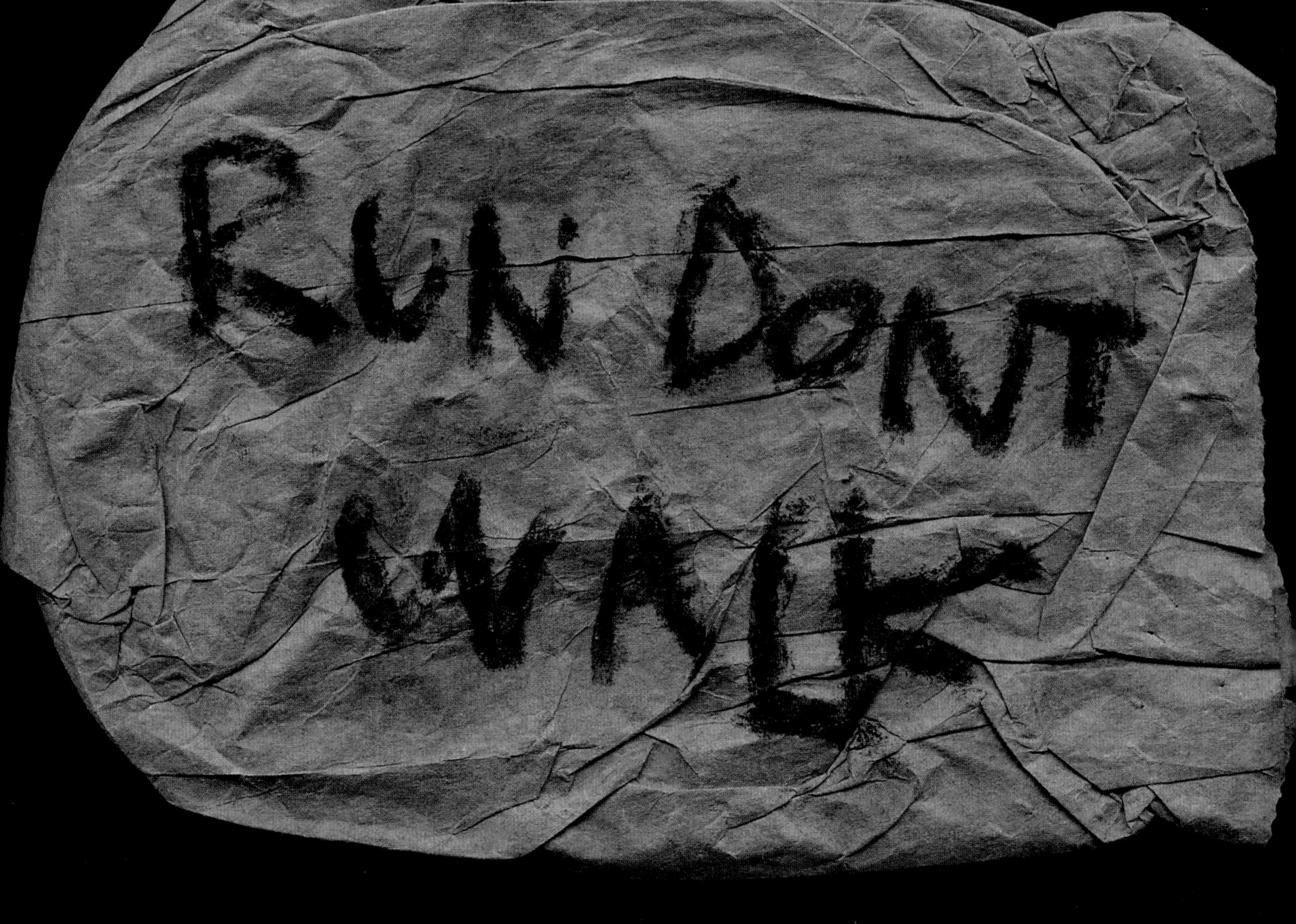
RUN DONT
WALK

my breath
has never
been
WORSE!
Extra®
Naturally and Artificially Flavored
SPEARMINT
Need a toothbrush
you could
1000s of

At least
as one of
them you pay
attention to me

INVOICE NO COMMENT
383916

AMOUNT DISCOUNT NE AMOUNT
25.95 0.00

CHECK TOTAL: 25.95

11Mark Economo Program

CHECK: 01312A

I WOULD LITERALLY KILL FOR SOME FRENCH FRIES

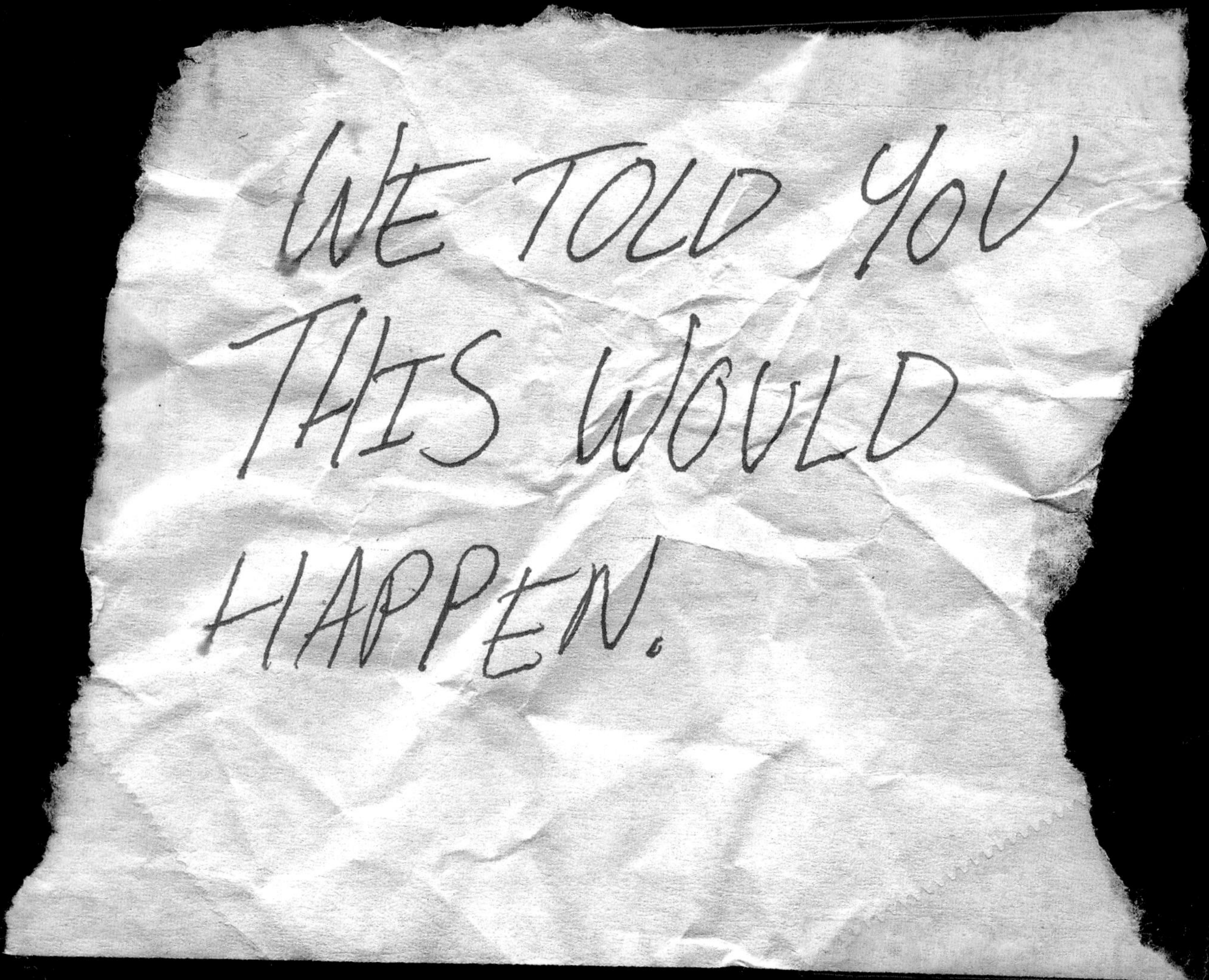
WE TOLD YOU
THIS WOULD
HAPPEN.

3 days. 3 days ago the outbreak started. 3 days the infection spread. 3 days is as long as I survived. I leave this simple list to you, my new friend, in the hopes that you don't repeat my mistakes.

- First, do NOT go to a church. I lost my family there, as well as my faith. God won't save you.
- Second, destroy the staircase! This may sound vague and I'd love to elaborate, but time is a luxury I don't have. When the time comes, you'll know what I mean.
- Third, loot. Fresh supplies are essential. Nobody is obeying the law anymore anyway. Why should you?
- Don't get your hopes up. Overly optimistic hope is your enemy here.
- Stay smart! Don't try to be a hero. There's no room for heroes in this new world and it only takes 1 mistake to end it all. Which leads me to...
- Don't let them bite you! They bite hard and trust me, it hurts.
- Now, this might be my most difficult piece of advice to follow. IF someone in your group is bitten, shoot them in the head. They're never the same after they get back up.
- You need to know this. They out number us 100-1. Can you really survive? Would you even want to? The best advice I can give you is this...

Press gun to temple.
Pull trigger.

If you find this I'm sorry. I was at Teresas. We were burning people at the end. Some of them weren't even sick! What did I do? God, I'm sorry

PRESENT DAY
I AM HUMANITY
I AM DEAD

To Whom It May Concern:

It was hard to do what I did. I had to barricade my door, block my window and — kill my brother. He was bitten. I threw up right after... because well — I saw the inside of his head. Not fun. I then had to take stock of all the supplies I had (good weapons, medical supplies, etc.). I managed to cut a peyhole in my attic so I could see outside. What I saw was Mayhem. Fire. People screaming, gunshots - the horrible sounds of Police sirens, morning —...it was horrible. Now everything has rattled down - I still hear gunfire but I'm used to it. If you live in Southern California, please start stocking up. I was barely able to survive in my city. I don't want anyone else to be added to the death count.

Did you see her
face?

Was that a
bite?

Her fuckin face
was half gone.

Let's stay
in here
Please

YA

Grant is slowing us
down. I think we
should leave him behind

NO KNOCKING!

ZOMBIES, No FUCKING JOKE.

I'm getting

really

sad.

LOOKING FOR AN INFECTED
WITH AN IRON MAIDEN
POWERSLAVE SHIRT. HE KILLED
MY FAMILY — I WILL TRADE
SEX FOR HIS LOCATION.

We got to the
manhole but
they were inside.
Rob was a bit. I
pushed him in to
get away.

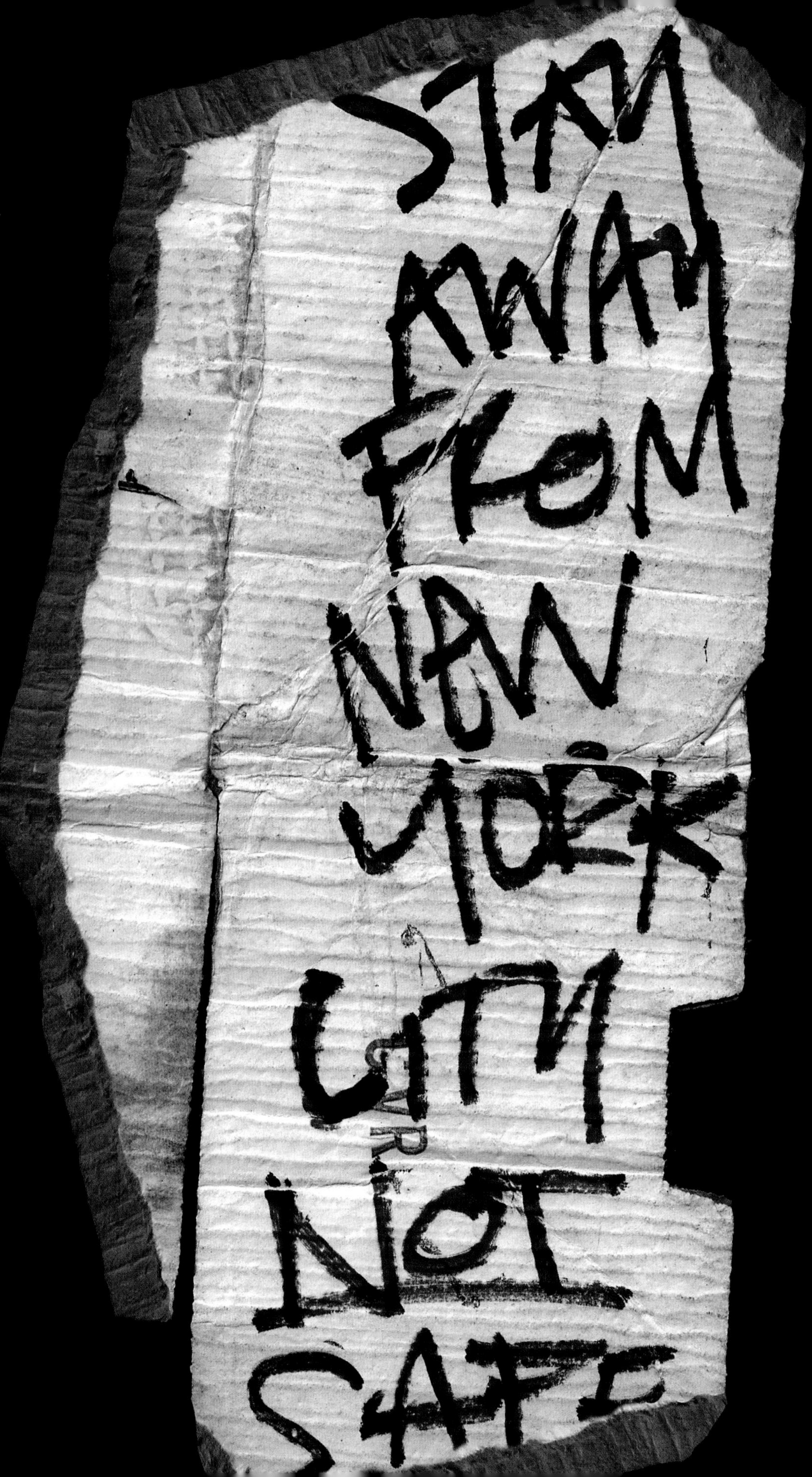
STAY
AWAY
FROM
NEW
YORK
CITY
NOT
SAFE

SLEEP

TIGHT

Dude!
I got the
espresso machine
working

FUCK YEAH!

I took a bunch of money from a grocery store. It has absolutely zero purpose but I keep thinking it will look good

if I meet up with a girl and casually pull out a wad of hundreds and say something like "I guess I don't need this anymore" and then I could light a fire with it

Journal Entery 31

At this point writting is the only thing keeping me from ~~testing~~ going in<u>sane</u>! today we sent scouts out looking for food and supplies. We havent heard from them in 10 hours. I think there dead but the others Still Hold out Hope. theres No Hope for Any of us we are All dead. We found out a few days ago that there Was maybe more survivors out the with a working website (Didnt think there would be anything left of the internet) we found a computer and sum wiz Kid got it working again with a old car battery and a wifi Hook up. god Damn its good to know every thing hasnt taken a Dump. But any ways we contacted the other survivors on the site but still no word yet But i Hope Soon I dont Know How much longer are battery supply will last.

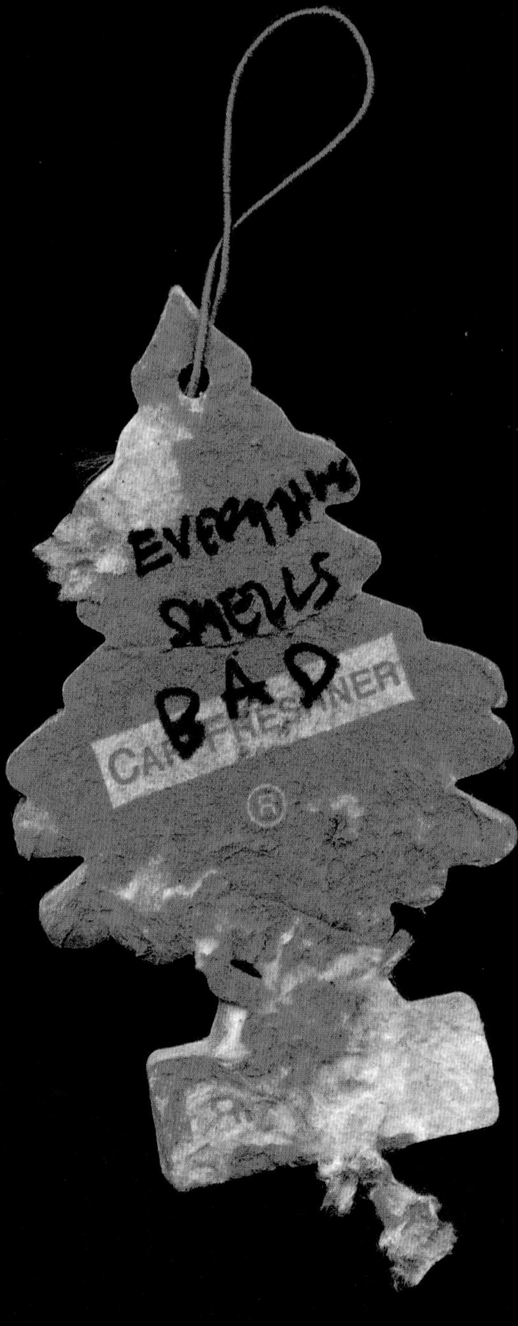
EVERYTHING
SMELLS
BAD

we ate the mushrooms

For the record you were
right, it was a bad idea

**bank.**

Officia

Member FDIC

Free online delivery of your monthly
checking and savings statements available.
Sign up today through Internet
Banking.

usbank.com

All of US serving you™

20133 (4/10)

00066 08884 0002 15
C/L PAY   **********9168
                              $445.00
                              "

I hope I get bit first so I don't
have to shoot any of my family.

I've lost track of the date. Yesterday screams filled the air. Missy — the puppy the boys found for Lynn — was killed by one of them. Lynn's screams drew more. I couldn't shut her up. I pictured my children dying. Trevor appeared and began shooting. Lynn passed out and we got her in the house. Zombies swarmed Trevor. There were too many. The dogs ran out to help him and they were attacked too. Mallory began screaming and they attacked the house. Becky came out screaming and it looked like she wanted those things to follow her. Some did. Then Mallory came out carrying the baby. She didn't get far. I swear she threw the baby at them. Did she? No she couldn't have. Charlie arrived too late. But he got all the zombies. It still feels unreal to use that word. I wish I could wake up from this nightmare.

Wake up!

do not track
infected
blood in
the house!

PERIOD.

Our Micro-Flex formula glides on and looks gorgeous all day.
Available in 30 shades.

DRAMATIZATION

Lets be serious, where the hell are we going to get a tank?

MICRO-FLEX KEEPS SUPERSTAY 24HR GORGEOUS...EVEN UNDER STRESS.

WITH MICRO-FLEX

WITHOUT MICRO-FLEX

I have to get this off my chest.

The woman, or should I say, girl, was obviously pregnant. She had been bitten and was bleeding down her arm. She was holding the bite when she walked up to me. "You have to help me!" She gasped, as she went down, hard, on her knees.

I had seen her walking up and down the road, next to my house, many times. She was Amish, you see. They don't believe in automated anything. She couldn't have been more than fifteen. One of the old men married her and got her pregnant right away. "Poor thing."

She looked at me pleadingly. I knew what I had to do, before she turned. I didn't know if it was to late or not, but I had to try, for her sake as well as the babies.

I took her to my house and gave her a powerful herbal drug to make her sleep. I tied her down tightly, said a strong prayer to the Goddess, and plunged a knife into her abdomen. The drug wasn't powerful enough, her screams peirced through my brain. I had to finish.

The baby was almost full term, when I pulled him out of the screaming woman. I cleaned his nose and mouth to get him breathing. I tied and cut the cord. He was a seprate being now. I took the knife, I had used to take the baby from the girl, and drove it into her milky eyesocket. Her screams and growls instantly quieted. Then the baby started screaming. I knew what I had to do. "Poor thing!" Goddess forgive me!

Wishing you holidays

that bring you together

with the traditions

and loved ones you cherish.

IT'S CHRISTMAS. BIT OF

A LITTLE I CAN HEAR

FEEL A THOUGH

I STILL, EVEN THOUGH

JOY, MEANING

THEM

This is just
as painful for
me too, George!

Please stop
talking to
the others
so much.

doesthis Seem
Weird to you?
like really weird

god and Santa
can i have
Mommy back

thanks

I made it through the
fires in San Francisco.
I crossed the Golden Gate
Bridge on foot while being
chased by these undead
fucks. I made it through
the winter. Grew my own
garden.

I was a Survivor

Now I'm gonna die from stepping
on a rusty ~~fucking~~ Nail.

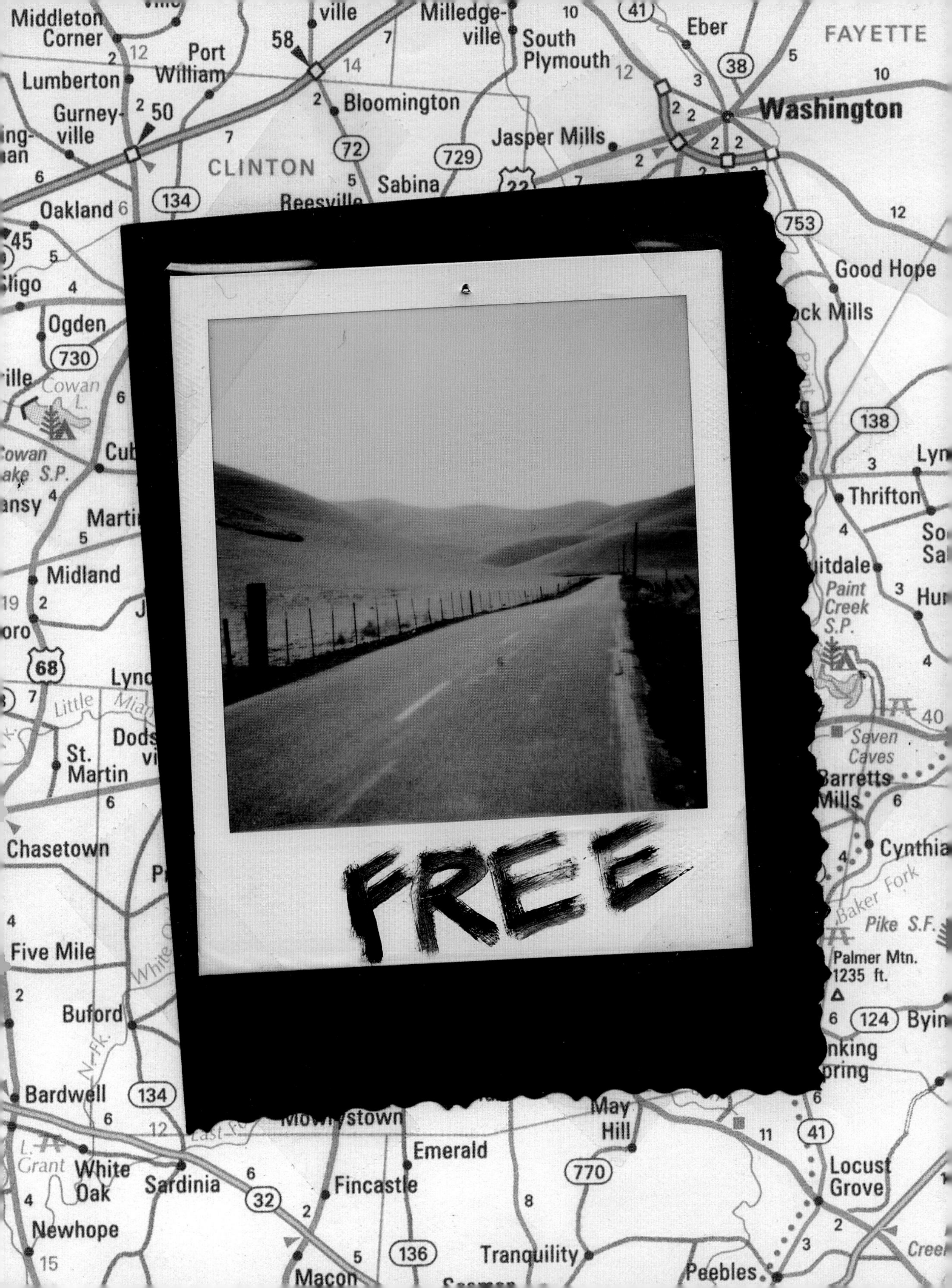
FREE
Middleton Corner
Port William
Lumberton
Gurneyville
Milledgeville
South Plymouth
Eber
FAYETTE
Washington
Bloomington
Jasper Mills
CLINTON
Sabina
Oakland
Good Hope
Ogden
Cowan L.
Cowan Lake S.P.
Thrifton
Midland
Paint Creek S.P.
Little Miami
St. Martin
Seven Caves
Chasetown
Cynthiana
Baker Fork
Pike S.F.
Palmer Mtn. 1235 ft.
Five Mile
Buford
Bardwell
May Hill
Emerald
White Oak
Sardinia
Fincastle
Locust Grove
Newhope
Tranquility
Peebles
Macon

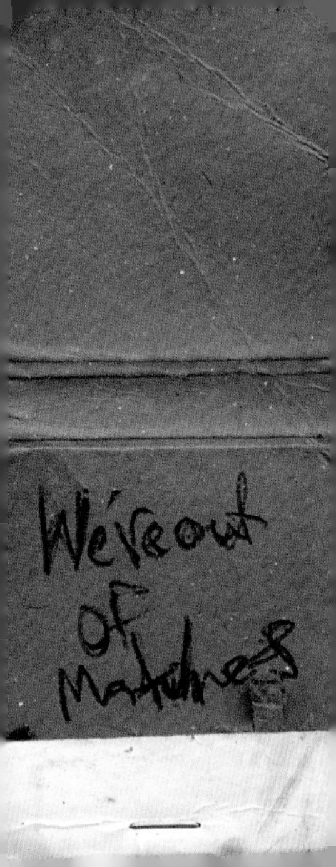
We're out
of
Matches

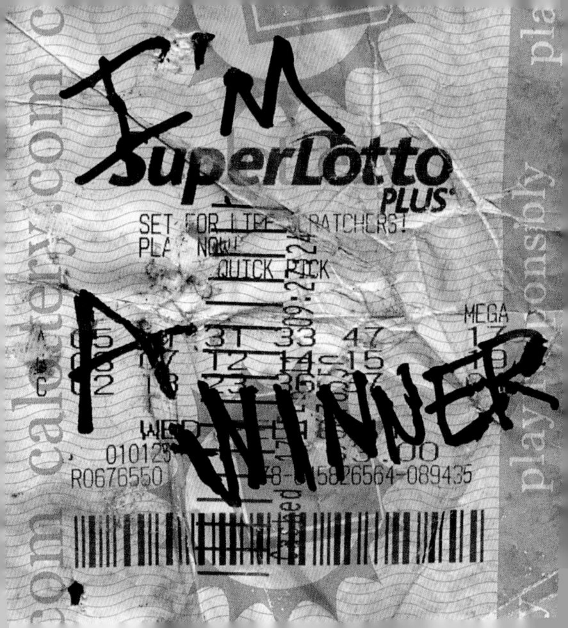
I'M
SuperLotto
PLUS
QUICK PICK
MEGA
A
WINNER
R0676550

This is the best thing that ever happened to me.

I'm finaly happy.

we're surrounded.
no food.
no water.

I love you

MEMO

IF your READING This PROCEED With Caution.

I was injured while trying to get Food.

I am Not sure if I am Infected, so
I have Quarantined MySELF HERE.
PLEASE Knock, If I dont Not Answer
Coherently→DO NOT HESITATE!
Shoot ME! I am No Longer a
Friend, a father, a husband, a human.

I Have Become DEATH. For Christ SAKE Shoot.
I Know I did my BEST Now You Do yours.

RUN, HiDE, Fight When you must...
But SURIVE
I'll miss you...
I LoveD you.

After killing my mother and sister because they became infected, I joined a group of survivors. Food became scarce and tentions were high. I broke out into a fight with a member and bludgeoned him to death with a rock.

Food was so rare, I decided to cook him up and eat him. The others don't know where he went and they don't know where I got the meat. They'll figure it out sooner or later.

I don't know if eating my comrad makes me just as bad as the zombies or if it makes me a stronger person. I choose to think I'm a stronger person, but once you get the taste of human flesh, it's never enough. I think I'll get into a fight next week too!

Shh... don't tell them any of this!

I'm tried.